SPANISH DRUMS

SPANISH DRUMS

Harry Chapman

MAINSTREAM
PUBLISHING

EDINBURGH AND LONDON

Copyright © Harry Chapman, 1991

The moral right of the author has been asserted
First published in Great Britain 1991 by
MAINSTREAM PUBLISHING COMPANY (EDINBURGH) LTD
7 Albany Street, Edinburgh EH1 3UG

ISBN 1 85158 319 X

A catalogue record for this book is available from the British Library

The publisher gratefully acknowledges financial assistance from the
Scottish Arts Council in the production of this volume

Typeset in Imprint by SX Composing Ltd, Rayleigh, Essex
Printed in Great Britain by Biddles Ltd, Guildford

Jacket author photograph © Sophie Baker

For my parents
Robin and Boo
With love and gratitude

'Spain never changes.'
                    George Borrow

'But another Spain is born . . .
With an axe in its avenging hand,
Spain of anger and ideas.'
                    Antonio Machado

Contents

PART ONE

RETURN TO TERUEL

1

The world was drowning. All along the coast the floods were spreading, destroying crops, furniture, turning the resorts of the Costa Brava into reservoirs of mud in which the fragments of people's lives – chairs, tables, boats they were paddling across their rooms to recover the remains of what belonged to them – floated at an aimless, watery speed. Fourteen people dead. Many more unaccounted for. The orange groves around Valencia a grey lagoon flowing towards the city and, up here, on the high plain of Teruel on the far side of the hills, more rain and no floods but a cold wind, the back walls of villages glimpsed beyond shivering trees.

It would have been easier if part of her body had not been dissolving. But it was her time of the month – and, seated at the back of the coach with the metal disc pressed into the palm of her hand, Ruth felt she understood why it had come a few days early. Her body's complaints – the sore lips and running nose, the pain piercing her with daggers, like the hearts of the Virgins in the south – were a necessary reaction, even the start of recovery. But Ruth knew that she must first get home – to work, peace, even dullness; the life she had been ready to leave behind.

Home . . . These piecemeal villages, these battered hills. The abandoned railway line with its derelict stations, one of which was drifting towards her across a field of pale green wheat.

The stations often reminded her of the civil war. This was ever since an old peasant woman had told her that General Franco had deliberately refused to have the line reconstructed, as a reminder and warning to the people of this region, which, for most of the conflict, had been inside the republicàn zone. For this was Teruel – province, city, battle in which 30,000 men lost their lives in the last winter of the war, in which men died of exposure and blood froze in their wounds. Ruth wasn't certain that the story about the railway was historically correct – and this mattered to her, but knowing it meant that every time she saw one of the stations, with its vacant windows and roof open to the sky, images of the war ran through her head like an old newsreel: troops waving from a train, men running bent double through olive groves, a line of refugees trudging out of the ruins of a city in the snow . . .

The war was her work and her romance, but now, in the receding station, she saw only the failure of her journey – its inner wounds, bombarded hopes.

She was seeing this landscape with the eyes of the stranger she really was. She had expected a different place, one in which the aridity of the land gave to rare islands of fertility – a vein of black poplars, the burgeoning of a fig tree over a wall – the value of water in a desert. Now the earth reminded her of someone who, after going for days without drinking, had lain down to gorge herself at a brackish well: it looked as sick as she felt every time the coach blundered into a pot-hole on the road, causing the disc of zinc to bite into the palm of her hand.

The coin was her return fare to this threadbare world, barely held together with a loose stitching of telegraph wires. It was anarchist currency: one of the tokens which the committees running the collectives which had been set up in the first months of the civil war distributed to their members, entitling them to 60 grams of meat, 100 grams of rice – depending on the village. The idea of the collectives, that agrarian experiment which in the end was destroyed by the communists on the republican side, had its own newsreel: municipal records burning in a village square, loaves stamped with the initials of the anarchist trades union, men dancing in church vestments in a grotesque distortion of the Mass . . .

The coach lurched off the road and the driver waddled off into a bar, leaving Ruth and one or two other passengers stranded on a muddy wasteland. Stillness. The wind battering the coach. The radio off so they could no longer hear the report of floods on the coast. And, through a patch on the misted-up window, a man with a moustache busily making *churros* at a stall.

Ruth stared as, scowling with concentration, he scooped white dough from a bucket and patted it into a syringe before forcing it through the ribbed spout into a spiral on a pan of simmering oil. He kept dunking the bubbly coil with a spatula until it was golden; then, inserting a griddle, shuffled it off on to a draining board and began to snip it with a pair of shears. Meanwhile, two or three small boys had been watching; now one of them passed over money for the 200 grams which the stall-owner weighed before tipping them into a paper cornet which he twisted at the bottom. The boy sprinkled sugar on the sticks, offering them to the others as he popped one into his mouth. Just behind him was a man with a side-drum hanging from his shoulder by a strap.

The drum struck her like an old memory, a lizard twitching on a wall. One drum-stick stood up from the man's belt while he trailed the other over the skin as if tracing a word in sand. The bud crackled on the taut surface; it was as though his arm were scribbling in a rhythm he did not control. He went on teasing the skin as a pair of civil guards strolled over in their capes and glossy black hats to chat to the man at the stall. But as the coach started to grind off he suddenly raised his head and began to drum, his violent tattoo blurred by a snare.

'So you came back to hear the drums?'

The woman on the seat next to her had turned as the coach once again began to sway. Ruth recognised the proprietress of one of the hotels in the next town – a coarse-skinned, angular woman with a cyst dragging down one eye-lid making her look half asleep.

She insisted, 'You'll be just in time to hear the drums.'

'I'd forgotten them,' Ruth murmured. 'But I don't want to miss them now.'

The mist drew back like a wisp of tissue-paper to reveal the town. She mouthed its name: Alcañiz, recalling that the Arabic word meant reed-bed; the main street rent the place in two, plunging down from the high *plaza* with a single kink in it – a lightning strike. To its right rose the rugged crag with the half-ruined castle – its silhouette drifted on the mist. And on the left the huge church with its roof of glazed tiles squatted turtle-like among houses of red brick.

Ruth couldn't suppress a smile as she saw the hotel proprietress beside her reading the tourist signs on the drab outskirts of the town, with their quixotic slogan: 'Alcañiz – Historic and Heroic City'. Heroic! The woman beside her with a bag of crockery wrapped in newspaper on the rack above. The coach driver scratching his bottom as he made his way over to the bar. It had occurred to her some time before that the sign said more about the vision of Spain propagated by the late regime than about Alcañiz's history, though perhaps the inhabitants had been inspired to some act of bravery on the occasion to which it referred: a siege in the war of independence against the French.

Suddenly they were charging up the dividing street, a feat to test any motorised vehicle to the limit. Wide-eaved houses flashed by – an old cake shop, the disused casino, the mysterious plaque commemorating the residence of Lieutenant Moore. The bus beached itself, an expiring whale, in the Plaza de España, and Ruth struggled off after the hotel owner, the strap of her bag grazing a familiar sore. As the coach swept past she suddenly saw herself standing in the same place on a summer's evening several years before, hearing the squeak of a rag as a barman polished the map of Spain under the arcade.

The square was a steeply raked rectangle like the deck of a galleon, low across the beam but rising at prow and stern. One end was dominated by the massive façade of the church of Santa María, whose empty interior – probably it had been sacked by the anarchists – had the air of a warehouse awaiting a delivery. From the balcony of the renaissance town hall hung a splendid rug emblazoned with the arms of the town – a castle between two maize stalks, because Holy Week had begun. And beneath the arches of a medieval market, a small sheet of paper was pinned to the door of the municipal library.

Ruth mounted the steps and read a typed message announcing the date of its reopening. Then she rang the bell. No one came. Bending down and levering open the letter-box she called out, but it was dark beyond the tiled floor and her voice came back. Behind her a whippet-like dog hoisted its leg against a wall.

Hearing a wayward clap of thunder, she hurried down a pedestrian street. Feeling the rain suddenly increase – it was dashing itself on the tiled paving, she stepped into a doorway to wait. It was the entrance to a shoe shop, one side of which was a mirrored wall. Somewhat reluctantly, she found herself in the glass.

Smoke-grey eyes. Straw-coloured hair. A face almost unlined – she was just twenty-three; yet she had caught age, she thought, in the last days as you might catch a cold – perhaps this was the effect of the blood-shot eyes, the sore beneath her nose. Although the features were the same, it was difficult to believe this was the enthusiastic postgraduate who had come out to live and work in this part of Aragón eighteen months before. She'd looked absurd then, for the sun had made her skin peel, revealing scraps of pinkness wrinkled like hot milk. It had bleached her hair, too, to an unaccustomed fairness, while she'd finally turned so brown that on her return to England at Christmas her friends had said she looked Spanish. This had thrilled her, though it was strange to have become foreign in two countries.

There was a sound like a steel hawser snapping under stress. For some time she had been aware of the chatter of a radio or television set above the roar of a vacuum cleaner coming from a balcony window above. Now the flood news had given way to a report on the forthcoming ceremony; there had been an abrupt cut to a group of drummers rehearsing. She imagined there must be five or six of them, for they were weaving a harsh tissue of rhythm from the high clamour of side-drums to the deep heart-beat of a bass drum. The noise swept the narrow street, developing, fading, returning.

For a moment – it was a twinge in her belly – she staggered just a little, fighting for breath; then the feeling had gone.

The rain was beginning to let up. Adjusting her bag, she crossed a square towards the building that was home.

2

His room was empty – it was as she'd expected, yet she couldn't repress a wave of disappointment: José's presence was so much a part of the peace she'd promised herself in the south. As her eyes wandered over the piles of books on his table, some of the pictures by which she constituted him flickered in her mind: the flare of a match within the parched darkness of the library, the sharp shadows cast by his features as he spread himself out, ravished by the sun, on the rocks above the reservoir.

Ruth found his absence reassuring because she knew the reason for it. Her irrational ringing of the library bell had reminded her that he was planning to spend Easter at the village house up in Belmonte, probably doing some of the repairs the place needed; perhaps, after fixing a socket or sanding a window-frame, he would have put up his umbrella and be strolling down to his parents' house for supper. Or he might be taking the van . . . Hoisting up a roller-blind she noticed that it was not in its usual place below in the square.

As she took a bath, letting the heat soak off dirt and pain together, she remembered driving out with him to help with the election cam-paign the previous spring. It had been an adventure, sneaking out at night to deal with an invisible enemy, for on the bend of a road the lamps of his van would catch a shimmer of fresh paste – the posters of a rival party. Quietly he would park so that in the glare of the lights she could see to dip the roll of paper into a bucket before he swept it up with a broom. Then, for a time – but not for long, for others would be following them on the road – the socialists' slogan 'For Change' and the fist holding a rose would obscure the messages of other parties.

It wasn't so much out of support for the socialist party that she helped José, although she was sympathetic to the idea of a moderate left-wing government, but out of a more general feeling that to join in with the campaign was to contribute to the re-establishment of democracy. During the dictatorship of General Franco political parties had been banned and the walls were clean as the streets, except for those government posters which boasted: 'Twenty-five Years of Peace'. Now faces, letters, symbols tore and blended on the walls; the plethora of initials by which the parties were known was reminiscent of the unstable period before the war. There was another argument, too, for backing the socialists – perhaps, indeed, this went some way to explain their relative success in the spring, which was that, as Spain had not had a socialist government since the time of the republic, its election would be a test of the resilience of the new democracy.

In her bedroom she opened a folder on her desk and took out a sheaf of papers. *Ruth Collier,* she read, *The Anarchist Experiment. A Study of Agrarian Collectives in Republican Spain 1936–1937.* It seemed to her that the words might have been written by someone else. In fact, she had barely begun her thesis – she was still doing the research, yet she had felt the need for a title and contents page, which served the purpose of those forests of wooden stakes supporting the floors of half-built flats. It was not due to laziness that her work was so unfinished: the transcripts of her interviews with old people who remembered the war and could be persuaded to talk about it filled another folder almost to breaking point. It was the way work seemed to breed work, so that the point at which she could sit down and start to fill in the gaps it created was continually postponed.

She moved a pocket cassette-recorder from the bed and got between the chilly sheets, lying still for a time while some herbal tea cooled in a glass beside her. As she climbed in something had made her switch the play button on. Now someone was speaking on the

tape – an old man telling of the proclamation of 'free love' by the anarchist committee in a local village, and his voice was like the con-
densation of all the voices she had heard and recorded during her stay
in Teruel.

She saw faces carved by the sun, their eyes watering with age, their
hands clenching and unclenching as they struggled with the dis-
tortions of time and fear. Sometimes the accents were so harsh –
cracked as the earth when the heat had sucked every bead of moisture
from it – that she had to ask José to help interpret the tapes when she
got back. Her attitude to her work wavered between a conviction of
the need for it and guilt at disturbing the peacefulness of age: the
men's long card-games on baize cloths in village bars, the knitting
and gossiping of the women on rush-bottomed stools in front of their
doors. Two or three times, when it seemed to her that the importance
of what a person knew overrode her reservations, she had recorded
secretly, from the pocket of her linen jacket.

She recalled how once, early in her stay in the town, she had gone
with José to the restaurant on the first floor of the hotel on the *plaza,*
and they had spoken of her work. Their affair had not begun, and she
had spent a lot of time in those days just watching him when he was
not looking at her, as if to justify in her own mind what it was in him
that she found so attractive.

José was a slim man, tall for a Spaniard and with the kind of lanky
body that looked best in a mackintosh or a dressing- gown. This
attracted her, of course, but more than anything it was the long sad
face – an El Greco saint's, she had once thought – which was so handsome in repose. When his mouth moved – to laugh or to chew a piece
of bread – his face lost its loveliness and became simply charming.
How can a person have two faces? she had once written in a notebook. *An adult's face and the face of a child?* And she remembered
how she had first been introduced to him, years before at the drums,
when adjusting the strap on his shoulder, he had put out his hand to
her, his face breaking for the first time.

Of course, he had other faces, too: the serene absence of sleep, the mask of anger or tiredness, when something had gone wrong at the library – but essentially there were these two. His face was like a subset of his character, for she had discovered that there were two José's; the first lively, dynamic, fired by his work, and the second subdued and inward-looking. They were reflected in his name, for what could be less solemn than the nickname Pepe, only strange if you had forgotten that José was the Spanish for Joseph, and that the same name was Giuseppe in Italian? José was rarely called this, for he discouraged it, but the pet name was always at hand when friends wanted to put their friendship to the test. Her own teasing took the form of referring openly to his two moods in terms of the bullring as *sol y sombra*.

It was *sol* that evening in the restaurant, for he was relishing something that had happened at the library. It was early days, people were beginning to discover the place, and a boy of eight, paying a visit with his class for the first time, had sidled up to his desk and whispered, 'Are we really allowed to take books home from here?' And he had described the severe middle-aged teacher who had brought them shaking her head with a sigh and saying, 'They never listen'.

His body seemed to glow with the success of the work he was doing.

'. . . So I'll put it to the mayor,' he was saying. 'You see over there' – he pushed back a net curtain to reveal the terrace of the library – 'you could fit in a couple, and then, if the mayor agrees, we can also use the ground floor of the town hall. Look, this arrived today . . .' He passed over the heavy book and she turned its glossy pages with their atmospheric photographs of rusted metal sculptures like the wrecks of warships at the bottom of the sea. In some of them the sculptor himself was at work.

'And you say you know him? How did you meet?'

'Oh, I don't know him well. But here and there – in Madrid. He's becoming very successful, and I think he deserves it – don't you?'

'With sculpture – it has to be there, doesn't it, before you can tell?'

After only three months there her Spanish still came and went, sometimes flowing so rapidly she was drunk with the exhilaration of it, at others dragging like a chain. Was the dissatisfaction she felt – the idea that her work had no practical value – no more than an expression of the fact that they still hadn't touched each other although they were becoming so close? That lack of physical contact seemed full of the menace of a hard dry wind which, if it were unleashed, might sweep away her questions like a bamboo hut blown down on the beach.

'It's because what I'm doing is so abstract. Dealing with the past . . . It's as though I were stuck in your library as it used to be – whereas you, you've been remedying it, it's a bright place now, and you can see smiles on the children's faces.'

'I admire your work more.'

She looked down at the piece of fish on her plate, and her hand trembled.

He went on, 'Helping to change people's points of view, the way they think about the past, for example, is a gradual process.'

'Your work does that, too.'

'By means of books such as the one you're going to write.'

She thought of an old woman she had interviewed that day who had broken down at the memory of some violence about which she would never be able to speak.

'And the old people – do you think I'm justified in troubling them?'

'Of course. We're not children. We've got to learn to face the past.'

I love you, she would write that night in her notebook, but what it was she loved – his way of putting things; unlike her he always thought before he spoke, the dry voice with its rustle of cicadas, or simply the moment when he had come into her life – she could not say.

'So you think a sculpture exhibition is a good idea?'

She looked through the book's dark pages, nodding. She sensed now that the balance of their relationship – her admiration for him, and the way he appreciated her work – meant that, if he wanted, they could go further, for they had arranged to share the flat as friends.

23

But a doubt still gnawed her: it seemed to her that her work was academic in the negative sense, and she longed for a way of progressing from theory to practice. She wanted to be like him not only in working for change, but in having some tangible proof of the work's value; not the scattered fragments of the past she faced alone in her room, but the excitement of unpacking crates of new books – above all the atmosphere of the library in the evening when it was a muted extension of the *paseo,* the cries of children playing hopscotch and the click of fans resolved into the rustle of pages and José's low murmur at the desk. Once she had tried to put these feelings into words and, although her Spanish at that moment had been hopeless, he'd understood, laughing at her earnestness. 'You're an English Quijote!' he'd said.

They had both laughed. And it was only later, after replaying the description of some atrocity the anarchists had committed, that Ruth had said to herself, 'Perhaps – but the stories which drive me mad are real.'

She supposed she must have drifted into sleep, for the camomile tea still stood in the glass by her bed, and the voice had changed on the tape. Gradually, as she came to, she realised what she was hearing; she had forgotten this recording – made at a lunch party down at José's sister Elena's house near the school for the purpose of testing her new cassette-recorder in the open air. The discreet black device had stood among the debris of food, an emblem of her foreignness. Yet it was at that lunch party that she had begun to feel that she had arrived in Teruel. The recording must have been overlaid with the interview; now it reappeared like water flowing beneath a hole in ice.

She could not remember how they had got on to the subject of the Easter drums. She heard her own voice, taut with nerves, say, 'There are two types of drum?'

Elena's voice said, 'That's right. There are side-drums, with a snare, which are played with two sticks – those are the light ones, and there are *bombos* which are played with just one big club.'

'You play a *bombo,* don't you?'

24

'Mm. Most of the women play side-drums because they're lighter, but *bombos* are easier. I think when my parents were young there were only side-drums – wait, let me ask my brother . . .'

She could see the table now – the clutter of lamb bones and plastic-topped wine bottles and a jar of peaches in syrup. They had gone on talking until late out on the terrace in a reddening sun; the white rect-angle of the school shivered through a screen of shaggy eucalyptus. Elena had turned to the others and suddenly two conversations had merged – it was all on the tape.

'Only side-drums?' – that was José. He was sitting beside her and speaking slowly; his voice sounded warm in the dusky air. 'Yes, the *bombos* came from another of the towns where it takes place – Híjar, I think.'

Ruth recalled the courage it had taken, in front of the four of them, to ask, 'And what about the origin of the ceremony? Does anyone know what it's for?'

There was chatter, the clink of a coffee spoon, then José again: 'There's a tradition that the drums represent the moment on Good Friday when the spirit leaves the body of Christ. "There was dark-ness over all the earth . . . and the veil of the temple was rent", and so on. In the Bible there are earthquakes, too, and rock-falls. Or it may be to do with frightening away evil spirits. There's recorded evidence of the ceremony in the eighteenth century, but then it fell into disuse and was revived in the twentieth by a curate called –'

Someone said, 'Mosén Vicente.'

'But only revived. They may have existed before the eighteenth century – maybe long before. Perhaps the Moors brought them from North Africa – Alcañiz is an Arabic name, or they're even older – an Iberian ritual. You only have to stand in the main square of Calanda at midnight on Good Friday and hear over five hundred drummers drumming together to feel how ancient it is. The fact that it's Easter – the time of the spring equinox – probably means it marks a transition between winter's death and the new life of spring. But what I like best about the drums is that they destroy time.'

Ruth reached out for the tape-recorder and pressed it off, suddenly repelled. She had not remembered the ceremony on her way back from the south, and now that she had heard a snatch of what was to come – the boy through the coach window, the group practising on the television – she hated the thought of that brutal celebration of noise which seemed intended to scare the earth out of its skin.

She remembered the flooded orange groves outside Valencia above which the train had crept along a causeway. She remembered her misery in the south. And she could not bring herself to imagine that it would ever end – this squalor of rain and cold and mud into which she too was dissolving.

3

The coffin was careering up the pavement on a two-wheeled trolley. The pale, unvarnished box was upright and a lot taller than the man in blue overalls who was pushing it with one hand while he steadied it with the other, like a reveller assisting a drunken friend home after a party.

Ruth had to stop for a moment and pretend to look into the window of a furniture shop before continuing down the street: it had taken her some time, even after seeing the empty coffin, to realise what it was. Her first instinct, she noticed with amusement, had been to cross herself – it was something the older women did on stepping in or out of their houses. Without that gesture to resort to she had simply waited for the shock to pass, realising it was not the thought of death which had alarmed her so much as the foreshortening of time. She remembered a sequence from an old film which had struck her as a child, in which the hands of a clock spun like a dervish and the sun and moon performed an ecstatic shuddering dance.

She had got up early that morning, intending to telephone José before he left his parents' house – she was prevented by pride, and had found herself sneezing as she buckled on her watch. Far from having recovered from her journey, she sensed that the process of unravelling its effects had only just begun; her period, too, still had a day or so to run.

It had stopped raining and she decided she felt well enough to go for a walk by the river. Descending the Calle Mayor – it was here that

27

she had met the coffin – she passed the old town club and a disused cinema, thinking how gloomy that area was with its high, rain-stained buildings and overhanging gables. At the iron bridge over the River Guadalope the water sounded like an orchestra tuning up. She lingered for a while, watching it rush through her reflection as if it were racing down a mountainside.

The dark river seemed to have a solidity the land lacked, running along the valley like a fault of metal ore, while in it and around it the long banks vanished and reformed. Whenever she saw the river it made her think of José, for it ran in counterpoint to his life: he had studied Law at Zaragoza University before returning to become librarian in Alcañiz. He had been born at Belmonte, a village up in the sierra in which, like a stone in a clasp, lay the reservoir in which they had swum when she first came to visit him. The sources of the river were even further up in the hills, in a landscape so calcinated that some of its inhabitants had necks goitred by the lack of iodine; above Belmonte, from the massive dam wall, a stiff chute gushed out to irrigate his parents' peach and almond orchards. Further down the valley it fed a second reservoir before joining the poplar-lined road to Alcañiz, where it hooked round the hills of the town, spreading out to the north beneath a viaduct of the abandoned railway line. Later it was swallowed by the Ebro as it slumbered past Zaragoza towards the sea.

The thought of the sea reminded her of a medieval Spanish poem she had read at school – something about our lives being rivers – but, before she could remember, a small pick-up truck slowed down, a hand waving from the window.

'Ruth! Ruth!'

She ran up to the old truck, hardly able to hear the driver's voice above the racket of the river. 'I've just tried your door-bell.'

The driver was Pedro, the son of a family who owned a cake shop in the town. He must have been nineteen or twenty, an outdoor person with a broad, attractive face who, apart from running his own car-repair workshop in competition with the big garage on the

Zaragoza road, helped to organise camping trips most weekends with children from the schools. His family took messages for Ruth and José, who had no telephone.

'What weather! I was just looking for you. Someone phoned.'

'Who?'

'Elena. She wanted to know if José was around.'

'No, he's away this week.'

'That's what I said, but I told her you were back. She said she'd try again.' Ruth thought she caught a trace of laughter in his eyes as he went on, 'You're back from the south, then?'

'As you see.'

'Weather remind you of home?'

She gave him a smile, all the same.

'I'm just taking a few things down to the workshop. Do you want to come for coffee?'

The tips of his fingers on the wheel were stained with oil. They drove into a muddy yard defined by a herring-bone pile of tyres; he carried an armful of hub-caps and a tool-box across the muddy yard, the bridge of planks squelching beneath his weight. They ducked through an iron door; Ruth felt honoured, but inside she saw that she was not the only guest. A boy of twelve or so, with brown shaving-brush hair and a pair of pebble glasses, was sitting on a swivel chair at a steel desk – Pedro's youngest brother, who gave Ruth his hand with disconcerting maturity. Beyond him a black and white television played shots of the floods: blocks of flats rooted in water, cars drinking through their radiators, a family paddling in a dinghy under an avenue of palm trees.

'Sixteen people dead!' the boy said brightly.

Pedro unloaded the hub-caps on to the floor.

'What weather,' he repeated. 'I was meant to be going on an excursion this week with the school – Elena was coming too – but it's been cancelled because of the storms. Run into any of the floods on your trip?'

'Outside Valencia, yes. It was like being on a boat. That was a reason,' she improvised, 'for coming back early. I missed the drums last year, so it'll make a change.'

She had seen his brother holding a side-drum on his knees. His finger-tips danced on it lightly, his face purple in the strip-light. He said, 'It's Pedro's. This year my father's going to get me one of my own. Pedro's promised to teach me.'

'Haven't you drummed before?'

'Only a child's drum. You should hear Pedro.'

The skins of the drum were transparent, like a block of ice. She could see the older boy now making instant coffee behind a glass window, holding the saucepan handle with a filthy rag. Beside him was a Savings Bank calendar with a picture of the Church of the Pilar in Zaragoza on it, minarets wavy in the stream.

'May I try?' Ruth asked. She took the strap and put it over her shoulder – it scraped the sore caused by her bag. On the skin the wooden sticks were explosive; they had a life of their own.

Bringing in the glasses on a tray, Pedro said, 'You're good. You should get one.'

She laughed. 'Perhaps I should. Will you keep it up all night?'

'I did last year. No – was it last year? The year before. My knuckles were bleeding – here and here.' He gestured as he handed her a glass. 'But this year I want to have a good time.'

'You're not in one of the church guilds?' She remembered hearing one of them – a group of twelve men – practising on the terrace beneath the castle. The sound had tumbled like the chips in a kaleidoscope.

He shook his head. 'My father wouldn't like it.'

There was a football match now on the television. The brothers compared teams as Pedro knelt down by a car, his tumbler of coffee on the floor behind him, trying the hub-caps for a fit. Ruth watched a fly land on his back and thought about his frowning concentration as he worked, his one-thing-at-a-time manner which inspired hope. The car was propped up at a tilt, its bonnet removed. In the stench of petrol, hearing the trickle of the drum, she thought: This is what I've come back to. Historic and heroic. This one-thing-at-a-time town with its vast empty church and the concrete stalls in the market with jars of giant olives and tubs of detergent. This – and my work, of course.

Suddenly she said, 'Can you lend me a car?'

Pedro stood up, wiping his hands. 'I don't know. How far do you want to go?'

'Not far. To José.'

'Up to Belmonte then? I suppose you can take that one if you don't want to go too far. It doesn't belong to anyone.'

He had nodded in the direction of an unpromising brown Simca with the names of a couple – 'Juan – Encarna' – taped over the top of the windscreen. A tiny plastic skeleton swung on a thread beneath the mirror.

'You're OK with the licence,' Pedro said, tapping the glass. She hadn't even thought of it. 'You've got a permit? Yes, of course. Hey, Luis!' he shouted to his brother. 'See if there's a key in that drawer!'

Five minutes later her idea choked and lived. She shouted over the revs, 'Don't you need me to sign something . . . ?' But Pedro was listening to each gear in turn, checking its tone; then he hauled back a metal door and drove the car out into the yard, one door flailing. She felt ashamed that her whim had been taken so seriously.

'No further than Belmonte,' Pedro said. 'She's not a hundred per cent. And don't overdo the speed!'

He and Luis stood waving in the doorway, just out of the rain. The road twisted and they were out of sight.

Just before the turning on to the Zaragoza road Ruth slowed down and unhooked the skeleton. Then she sat there with the car's engine running, wondering if it were wise to drive off like this. Would José mind if she turned up without warning? She knew she had troubled him by her decision to go south, quite how much she wasn't sure. Perhaps to appear unannounced would be a mistake? But it was too late; the plan was in motion; the car made it difficult to change her mind. As she turned off the main road the two hills of the town

31

parted company behind her.

Later she came out of a tunnel beside the reservoir. It was full now, of course, and choppy with the rain which blurred the distinction between its edge and the hills which rose sharply from the far shore. The road ran along a shelf on this side; the presence of the water, now, was vague and undefined. She remembered her first visit to Teruel when she and José had swum there in water so clear you could see without distortion down to your feet. She had felt the unnaturalness of it then, the abruptness of the shoreline which revealed it was man-made: José had told her that a whole village had been evacuated and lay beneath; when they were children he and his sister had once gone out to look for it in a stolen boat.

She found the handle for the window and wound it down; a curtain of rain brushed her face; suddenly she heard a rattling noise coming from the far side.

Was she mistaken? Curious, she stopped the engine and got out. The wind raced across the water's surface, leaving huge birthmarks; she mounted the high wall at the edge of the lay-by and walked along it.

Silence. Wind in the fennel by the road. The rattle again. Someone was practising on a side-drum, probably at an open window in the stone house on the far side. The brittle hard sound crossed the water; the echo made her look round, for it seemed as though a ghost-drummer were replying from the cliffs above.

She returned to the car and drove on, leaving the solitary drummer tapping out messages to himself across the water.

4

Dear José,

I'm writing this in a steamed-up bar just off the Plaza Mayor after *churros* and coffee. Sorry about the paper – I've had to tear a page out of my notebook. Today I've been a real tourist. This morning I went to the Prado (from which I send the enclosed card – I didn't know Velázquez painted landscapes, did you?) and then for a walk in the Retiro, which felt like spring although there are no boats or pedalos yet on the lake. Last night I tried to get into a production of Lorca's *Mariana Pineda* at the Teatro Real, but no seats were available. I suppose you're working on the new catalogue, so I'm sending this to Alcañiz hoping to catch you before you go up to Belmonte. Don't work too hard!

I promised I'd write from here and give you some idea of how I'd be feeling at this stage of the journey. Really, though, so little has changed since we talked there hardly seems anything to say. I'm catching the train south from Atocha station at ten this evening. I still don't know what will happen. But I promise you I've told you the truth. He has another girlfriend, and I don't think that either of us – really – knows how we feel about it. I just wish –

I suppose it's wrong of me to feel that you might find it upsetting that I should even feel a need to 'make sure' after what's happened; certainly you've never actually told me straight out that you might feel pain about it. That evening last summer – I'd wondered for so long about whether it might happen, and it seems incredible now that we should have waited so long – when you kissed me the first time, I told you I didn't know what it meant, and you said you understood. Now I'm not sure if you do or not, or even if uncertainty is something a person should accept, let alone demand.

Why am I mentioning this? Only, I suppose, because often when I think about all this I feel ashamed. Yet it seems clear to me that – as you yourself said – I must try to decide exactly what my feelings are before going any further. My excuse is always to have told you the truth. But perhaps that isn't enough?

Please forgive me, and thank you for being so understanding.

Love,
Ruth

She turned the letter over in her hands, shaken by her own hypocrisy. For the first time she was conscious of one of the worst side-effects of a base act – that it inhibits a person's future actions; she felt she had relinquished her right to expect him to come back. What was more, she had always imagined that honesty was one of her strengths. How then could she have been sincere and at the same time so double?

Well, she had been punished on the journey. And I'm still being punished, she thought, sitting on the unmade bed in the house in Belmonte in which José had slept.

She sat back against the mahogany headboard, hearing it creak, and looked at the postcard with its dim cypresses. When she had first picked up her letter – its blue and red striped border had stuck out from the pages of a book beside the bed – her handwriting on the envelope had looked like a stranger's. Was that how José had felt on receiving it? Opening it, she had felt as if she were spying on someone, as if a letter, after being sent, belonged exclusively to the person who had received it.

Suddenly she had an image of herself in the south: her tear-stained face in a sloping mirror above the marble table at which she was miserably stirring a coffee. She pressed the letter fiercely to her breasts, thinking: Poor me. Poor José. Poor Tom, even.

She felt herself blushing as she replaced it in the envelope, then picked up the book. It was not from the library as she'd expected, but a frayed paperback copy, in French, of a book whose title, *Reflections on Violence,* seemed familiar – perhaps she had seen it in some bibliography or other? Opening it, she saw in large round hand-writing the words: *Juan Alejos Utiel – Paris 1969.*

She recognised the name of José's elder brother, who had died after a demonstration in Madrid several years before. She knew very little about what had happened, for the fearless interrogator of strangers felt she didn't know José well enough to press him on the subject; besides, he hated to talk about it. All he had told her were the bare facts that, after being arrested, his brother had died from injuries sustained in the demonstration, or – but there was no proof of this – as a result of torture by the police. Once – they were returning from the showing of a Spanish film at the town theatre – she had tried to lead him on from a point raised by the film to saying more about it, but he had snapped at her, demanding that she did not ask again. And although she was disappointed she didn't resent this, for she sensed that even if they were closer it would be the same; he did not speak of it to himself.

Ruth could not be certain, but she suspected that, on the two or three occasions – there were no more – when, without warning, he had fallen into a mood of unmitigated gloom, he was thinking about his brother. In this state he was immune to signs of sympathy. *'Sombra?'* she might ask softly, in an attempt to raise a smile, but this mood was darker than shade, a tyranny of silence from which her presence was ruthlessly banned. He would not even shake his head if she suggested a walk; yet later she would see him trudging down the street in the blazing sun, on his way to fight a duel with depression on the dusty sheep-tracks where the shadows were sharper than knives.

So she had made do with the two photographs of Juan she had seen: the formal studio one of a young man with a parting on his mother's dressing-table, and the snapshot of a much older child standing behind two young ones at a picnic by the reservoir.

The consciousness of José's absence entered the room. At first she had told herself he had probably driven into Calanda to buy something for the house: she had passed a couple of paint-pots on sheets of newspaper where he had been painting the hall, but the paint was dry. Now she realised that although the bed was unmade there was no suitcase, nor were there any clothes in the wardrobe; in fact apart from the book there was nothing of his in the room at all.

The front door of the house had been open when she mounted the steps. She had wondered if José's mother was inside, remembering that she had a key and came in occasionally to do a little housework, although the house now as good as belonged to José and his sister. But there had been no one – only the squeaky hinge of a shutter and an empty packet of Ducados on the kitchen table.

She was not used to being alone in the house. She remembered it as being animated, always, by the hiss of frying oil, by Elena's untrained voice singing loosely to a guitar. Now it was as though it had fallen asleep, the only sound within, the tinkle of the tiny chandelier in its linen bag in the oval dining-room.

She swept back a fallen mosquito net and stepped out on to a terrace. The house was at the top of the village, its back wall set into the hill which rose steeply up to the remains of a castle on the crags above; from where she was standing she could see through the ruins of an abandoned house to a terraced orchard of peach trees descending to the breach of poplars below. The wall of the dam stood at eye-level so that the surface of the water could not be seen. But whenever she saw that wall of reinforced concrete she felt the sheer weight of its pressure against the dam.

On the terrace was a pair of sodden wicker chairs beneath a rusty wire pergola. Looking back at the chairs she could see the five of them sitting out there one evening around a paraffin lamp planning a hike up into the Pyrenees. She remembered that trip as a series of overwhelming physical sensations: the tug of the straps of a rucksack on her shoulders, the icy taste of the stream falling like a rug over the wall of rock from which they had sipped on their way up the long valley.

It was one of the times when she had felt at one with herself and José. Up there in the wild silence of the mountains her troubles were replaced by more basic difficulties: the ache of her legs, climbing the slope; where to find enough kindling for a fire above the tree-line.

As he was older than the others there was an unspoken understanding that José's cousin Eduardo was in charge of the expedition. Ruth had disliked him at first, for unlike the others he had not seemed to be able to take her at face value: he was continually goading her with feeble jokes about England and Englishness. On their way up the valley – she and José had got ahead of the others and stopped in a shaft of sunlight to drink the whisky she had brought – José had said, 'Don't take anything he says to heart. Eduardo's got problems.'

Ruth was taken aback, for apart from the teasing, which seemed to be his way of coping with her distinctness, she had thought of him as affable, if a little conceited.

'Has he? What sort of thing?'

'Oh, this and that. He'll get over it for sure.'

She had pressed him on the subject, but José would say nothing; she put this down to the solidarity of Spanish men towards each other – she knew how *machista* they were, even if, like José, they did their best to deal with it. That night she had woken in the refuge to find the sleeping-bag beside her empty and heard the murmur of the two men as they sat by the fire. When she got up their voices dropped; instead of going back to bed she grabbed her coat and went out to where the great mountain reservoir at the top of the valley lay under a hair-line moon. And out in front of that expanse of darkness she had clenched her nails into her palms with frustration at her separateness.

37

Leaving the terrace, she entered a dim room in which the striped wallpaper was puckered on the walls. In the light from the panes in the door she saw the old music on a piano with two ends of candles in brackets; wax had dribbled on to the keys. Albeñiz, Granados, Ravel – Elena sometimes played.

With a few fingers Ruth picked out a folk-song she knew; her left hand stumbled over the experimental harmonies of Lorca's arrangement, made stranger by the jangle of the old upright. She even sang hoarsely:

'The moon is a little well,
Flowers are worthless
All I value are your arms
Embracing me, at night. . . .'

Suddenly she turned, feeling she was being watched. The window was open, and a gust of wind flustered the bobbled swags of a pair of curtains.

She was used to the house being inhabited, she thought now, not only with living beings but the presences with whom it was peopled by her imagination; José had told her that as a child he and his brother and sister had liked to dress up there in the old clothes they found, ambushing one another in the endless telescope of its rooms.

For the house seemed to be a series of alcoves which were joined on to one another in unexpected ways, as if each pair of doors in a panelled wall led into another era of Spanish history. The house had the usual quota of stories, too, which accumulate in old buildings, as if the passions and sufferings of the people who have lived within become a part of the architecture. There were tales of nuns having been built into the walls as a penance, of frescos of the New World concealed behind thick layers of wallpaper, of silver stored in the foundations to keep it safe from the French. José had even told her of a tunnel leading from the cellar up to the heights of the castle above, which had provided the means for raising a siege by allowing the besiegers to enter the castle precincts secretly, at night.

This was supposed to have occurred during the first of the Carlist wars, which were a premonition of the conflict which provided the background to Ruth's studies, in which a liberal government faced rebellion by the forces of reaction. Even the bed of that war's great liberal general, Espartero, was to be seen in one of the rooms – a nineteenth-century extravagance of gilded wood.

She was distracted by an old print over the piano. It was foxed, but beneath the stains she could make out a North African scene: a few white round-roofed houses, the spikes of palm trees, a pair of camels. Seeing the room reflected in the glass she suddenly asked herself how these things had survived the requisition of furniture by the anarchists, the burning of bourgeois artefacts on a bonfire in the village square?

The air of the cellar was muffled by the sandy floor. She was surprised at how dry it was; there was no sign of fungus or even damp behind the wooden shelves with their medicine bottles and bunches of dried arnica and camomile. A row of earthenware oil-jars bulged in a wooden rack, their cork stoppers in place; a warping mill stood in a corner. Beyond some brick pillars lay a room whose ceiling was of rock. A dark still-life of dead game leaned against a table; on this was an inlaid box containing an ivory paper-knife and some books bound in calfskin, one of which she untied and opened – it was Latin. On a chest lay an old quince-jelly tin with an art nouveau woman on it; beside it was a pile of red bound volumes of an illustrated magazine of the twenties. Ruth glanced at the engravings: a vessel of the Spanish navy, a Sevillian barber's shop, a portrait of Alfonso XIII. Somewhere behind her stood the huge sideboard which, José had told her when he brought her down here, concealed the entrance to the tunnel – she had wanted to see, but there was so much junk in the way he'd persuaded her that it would take a whole day to move it. Then she saw the trunk.

It was of battered leather reinforced with wooden batons and stuck with shipping labels for many countries. She dragged a threadbare blanket from the top, then lifted the clips; the heavy lid yawed as the leather hinges took its weight. The box was full of straw; as the dust from it rose she smelt the warm fragrance of summer. A little gingerly, in case there were something living beneath, she put her hands in and drew out a worn pair of working-men's trousers, a collarless shirt, a scrap of lined paper on which, in a big careful hand, she made out the words: 'and if you can, some more butter and chocolate'. Beneath this was a layer of old newspapers.

She reached down and, moving these aside, brought out a steel-blue forage cap with a red tassel lying on a studded suitcase beneath. She unfolded it and stood it on the table; then, extracting the box – it was about the size of a backgammon set, she opened the catches and saw the saddle-leather of a bone-shaped object lying among some torn rags. Unbuttoning the holster she took out a hand-gun and laid it, heavy and cold, across her hand. It had a primitive look: an arrangement of circular hinges along the breech reminded her of a model railway locomotive. The work *Gesichert* was stamped above the grip.

Ruth felt her breath coming at a faster rate; she was conscious not only of her fear but of an awful sensation of power which had crept up on her unawares. She resisted the desire to scream. As her hand held the gun its weight seemed to grow so that she had to rest her wrist on the edge of the trunk to support it. She waited for her breathing to slow down; then her hand opened and the thing fell as if it had jumped on to the sandy floor.

She was just reaching down to retrieve it when she heard the creak of a wooden beam above, and a voice calling, 'Is anyone at home?'

5

Elena said, 'My brother told me you'd gone south.'

They were seated in the kitchen finishing the bread, cheese and salad which Elena had been down into the village to buy. The wind had gathered strength again and was flapping a loose shutter some-where; outside, beyond the ruined wall, a thicket of fig-tree branches creaked. The hatch down to the cellar was at Ruth's back, in a pantry adjoining the kitchen.

'The south? Yes, yes – I did go. But I came back early . . .' She wondered if José had told his sister her real reason for going. 'It's my time of the month and I was catching this cold.' It had made the cheese taste of nothing. 'I wasn't spying on anybody, Elena – I really wasn't. I don't know what I had in mind.'

'Did you find anything down there?'

'Well, yes, I must admit . . . I was a bit taken aback. Did you know there was a forage cap and' – she swallowed – 'a gun . . . ?'

Elena nodded. She was smoking an American cigarette, and as she exhaled a hooped earring vanished behind a trace of smoke. José's sister was some years older than Ruth, but her features were of the kind which tauten but do not fade; Ruth envied her dark gold hair and large eyes which occasionally – it was like the transition, within a piano chord, to a minor key – had the lovely mournfulness of José's.

She had known her longer than her brother, for Elena had been going out with one of the sons in the family Ruth had stayed with in Madrid during the year abroad which formed part of her course at university. In those days – it was shortly after Franco's death – Madrid had been a restless city, its streets cordoned off or full of people running from the distant phut of tear-gas canisters; Elena had shown her the place where, some years before, a terrorist bomb had killed Carrero Blanco, Franco's intended successor, blowing his car over the roofs into the courtyard of a block of flats. A book shop they passed had had its windows shattered by right-wing vigilantes because it stocked the works of Marx. The young man Elena was going out with called himself an anarchist – the word meant little to Ruth in those days, though she could see in a general way that the Spanish people were coming to terms with things which had been prohibited for forty years; while she was there Santiago Carrillo, the exiled leader of the communist party, returned and there was talk of Spain now fulfilling the conditions Picasso had laid down for the transfer of *Guernika* to the Prado.

In the flat where Ruth stayed in the Atocha district, the walls of the self-proclaimed anarchist's room were covered in poems by Neruda and Picasso doves; the inevitable Che Guevara hung in transfiguration on the door and, as they sped out of Madrid towards Teruel in his open car, a song by Paco Ibañez – the hoarse protest singer – unwound like a banner of defiance to the blind hills.

The two girls had not become friends. Perhaps it was because she was older that Elena had made Ruth feel one step behind, so that the Spanish girl's generosity – showing her Madrid – was in itself a reason why they did not become close. Perhaps it was Ruth's emotional caution which made her fear Elena's temper, her barricade radicalism, her pot-smoking friends; until that spring Ruth had cherished another image of Spain, one involved, she began to realise, with the ideology of the dictatorship – a Spain of old-fashioned virtues, of *honor* in the austere setting of Castile.

Of course, Elena had grown up. She would laugh now, Ruth was sure, if reminded of that time, yet like many people whose youth has been spent exploring and demolishing emotional barriers she had become unspontaneous, her attitude to life characterised by an impatience increased by her failure to establish a permanent relationship. She was modern; she was alone. Was it merely some instinct of self-preservation that had once made Ruth determined to hold on to innocence – all her life, if possible – although it seemed to her now that her decision to travel south had removed the last shred of that pretence. Perhaps she and Elena had something in common after all?

She expected her to explain the gun – to say why they had allowed it to remain among all the other stuff cluttering the space below; instead Elena smoked on, combing her stiff hair with her hand, toying with a piece of chocolate she had snapped off a bar lying on a plate. 'And if you can,' Ruth thought, 'some more butter and chocolate.'

She asked, 'So did you see José when he was here?'

'No, it was earlier, in Alcañiz. He said he might be coming up. At that time I still thought I was going camping with Pedro and a group of children at the school. Then that had to be cancelled because of the weather . . .'

'Perhaps he's at your parents'?'

'No . . . I called in just now on the way to the shop, but they said they hadn't seen him since yesterday. They thought he was here, too. These men – ' She broke into a smile.

Ruth suggested they go out for a walk.

In the street it felt warmer, although still damp; a flash of sun glittered in the puddles on the road. They descended the steep street and then wound down to the river below the dam. They could hear the chute tumbling out at full pelt as they strolled along the bank under the bare trees. Soon the track forked and joined another, and the river was all around them, rushing along beneath the silver trunks so that it was impossible to distinguish the chanting of the stream from the wind in the branches. The stones beneath the water were glossy, like an inlaid chessboard.

'I've been trying to get in touch with my cousin,' Elena shouted.

'Eduardo? Isn't he in Zaragoza?'

'Doesn't seem to be. I tried to ring to tell him about my trip and to ask him if he and his wife were coming up here for Easter – but I tried three or four times yesterday and this morning and each time I got the engaged signal. It's as if he's unplugged the phone.'

She bent down and picked something up.

'Did you think he might have come up here?'

'I thought José might know.'

She skimmed the pebble across a section of the stream: it grazed the water six or seven times before plopping in. They had come out as far as they could go along a ridge of white stones, leaving the watery thicket behind. Further on, the river vanished over a straight edge of rocks below which could be seen the dull haze of birches and aspens.

Elena said, 'Things have been going badly for Eduardo recently.'

'In what way?'

'Hasn't José mentioned it?'

'Only about a drink problem. But I thought –'

'Yes – that seems to come and go. There were drugs, too – but he's through that stage now. You know a couple of years ago he tried to kill himself?'

'My God.'

'He tried to jump in front of a train at Atocha station. Luckily someone had the presence of mind to grab him. Of course, all he succeeded in doing was frightening his wife.' Her tone was impatient.

'And what was the cause of it? Did it have something to do with his work?' She remembered that Eduardo was a sound engineer for a local radio station in Zaragoza; once, when they had been in the city, he had shown her and José around the studios.

'Oh, no, no,' Elena said. 'This last job seems fairly stable. No, Eduardo's problems are more connected with his family – with my family, I mean. His father died when he was fifteen. I don't know much more about him because we've never been close. He's so much older than José and me. By the time I was at boarding school Eduardo was already in his last year at Madrid University.'

Ruth said – it was a line she had used in her interviews, 'Things must have been so different in those days.'

She had not expected the flow of Spanish which poured out, as

Elena's words moved from thought to thought across what she knew of her cousin's history. Ruth watched as piece by piece, in the course of her speech, she stripped the bark of a thin birch wand until it was green and bare, crushing the carapace between finger and thumb. She spoke of Eduardo joining the communist party – still illegal in those days, of his involvement in printing and distributing literature, in student demonstrations, in contacting party members in exile. She told Ruth how, because of his drink problem, he had lost his job at Radio Televisión Española; how it had taken him several years to find another job. She described how, when she was at university in Madrid, she had tried to get to know him better – as a schoolgirl she had admired him for his political work – but that Eduardo was distant and hostile. 'That was when you were in Madrid,' she said.

Ruth listened and thought. Until then she had associated the Spanish communist party – she had not known Eduardo was a member – mostly with the period she was studying, when it had mounted a campaign against the anarchists which had finally resulted in the dismantling of the collectives. Now she tried to fit Elena's report of her cousin's youth with her own childhood glimpses of the dictatorship: a line of black taxis with red stripes waiting outside the glass doors of Barajas airport; policemen elegant in grey and red. She remembered the rows she had witnessed between Elena's boyfriend and his mother in the dark old flat near the station beneath which the trains clanged and hooted in the night, their wheel-sparks flashing blue on the moulded ceilings. She remembered a group of demonstrators charging into the severe geometry of the Plaza Mayor waving a red flag – that day the communist party had been legalised.

'Was Eduardo ever in prison?' she asked.

'Yes, once. A couple of years after his father died I got this phone call from a friend to say he'd been arrested. He'd been involved in a demonstration and he'd been taken somewhere – Lérida, I think. My mother and I drove up to visit him. I can still remember that journey – it was misty and everything was white, white, white. We spoke through a wire cage and I remember him telling us that they wouldn't let him smoke. He was let out quite quickly – there wasn't enough evidence to convict him of anything.'

Ruth said, 'And is he still a communist?'

'No, he isn't anything. I don't think he voted in the last elections – he's got this notion that the people around him are betraying something. And of course now democracy's here, it's harder to know who are your friends and who are your enemies.'

She tossed the switch into the stream, where it turned on its axis before catching in a tangle of twigs.

'It isn't only me who says things are going badly for him. It's his wife. Teresa says he's so moody – and he won't tell her what's on his mind. Only she's patient about it – I wouldn't be . . . It's starting again.'

The rain was pricking the stream. Ruth felt a drop on her brow as they hurried back along the path between the trees.

It was only when they reached the steps of the house that she spoke again. 'Listen – that gun I found –'

'It belonged to my uncle.'

Ruth knew not to ask more. It was something she had learned from her interviews – the tone which said – 'Enough', concealing the knowledge of slaughter. She followed Elena up the steps into the panelled hall.

6

The sun had set behind deep clouds, as if withdrawing into the
interior of a cave. As they crossed the river and spun along the road
beside the park Ruth remembered her walk down there that morning
and meeting Pedro on the road. It was like the rewinding of a tape:
there, behind a row of dank cypresses, stood the padlocked door of
the workshop; they passed the place where she had paused,
uncertain whether to drive on.

Elena had appeared up at the flat a few moments before to invite
her to supper. At first Ruth had hesitated, feeling unwell; then, faced
by the emptiness of José's room when she went in to pull down the
blinds, she had changed her mind. As they set off Elena handed her a
plastic bag of cassettes out of which she chose one of a singer who did
settings of modern poems. He sang to an acoustic guitar:

> 'Of all the stories in history,
> The saddest, without a doubt, is that of Spain,
> Because it finishes badly –'

The words were as out-dated as the style.

Elena lived in a row of bungalows which framed three sides of a
courtyard in which an old gas canister on a high dais and a number of
water and electricity installations lay like discarded artillery among
nettles and long grass. The bungalows had been built in the thirties
as accommodation for teachers at a school which had been replaced
by the present concrete and glass boxes which were visible through
the screen of eucalyptus.

They had driven through a sort of no-man's-land where white-washed walls backed on to a neglected nectarine orchard and a row of small villas appeared through a fence of cypress, the trees' joints oiled by the rain. Standing on the terrace as Elena fumbled with the lock Ruth remembered the lunch party at which she had tested her tape-recorder; looking back at the muddy courtyard it was difficult to imagine the day in September when they had sat out on the terrace seeing the light soften over the rusted machinery lying in the yard.

Suddenly a voice came from a gap in the buildings and a short, stocky woman stepped up on to the terrace with a carrier bag.

'Elena, is it you? I saw a light on. Oh, there you are!'

'Teresa!' Elena cried as they kissed her. 'What are you doing out here? Are you all right?'

'I tried to ring but you were out.'

'I tried to ring *you*. Have you unplugged your phone?'

'I'll explain. . . . Who's this?'

'José's friend, Ruth – you remember.'

'Of course – Ruth. It's so dark out here.'

Teresa kissed her on the cheeks; as a bulb blazed Ruth saw her straightforward, not-quite-pretty face, its healthy complexion drained by the light. Ruth had liked Teresa on the trip up to the Pyrenees; she was more forthright than the others, perhaps because she had not been to university, and even harsh in a way that for some reason made her seem vulnerable. The others teased her for being a chatter-box; in fact, she just spoke more loudly and with more enthusiasm about everything – she had horrified them on the drive north with gruesome stories about the clinic where she was a nurse. Meeting her alone for the first time, Ruth realised to what an extent she had thought of her as a part of – a support for – Eduardo: perhaps that was how Teresa saw herself?

She left the bag in the hall, propping it against the skirting-board beside a framed reproduction of Dalí's *Crucifixion*. Elena shared the house with two other teachers so that parts of it – the hall, the kitchen and dining-room – contained an amalgam of different furnitures: the place never seemed to settle down. The others were away now; those parts of the house dank and empty. But Elena's living-room was homely enough, with a spare bed and one of the walls covered with a striped rug.

As Elena passed round a dish of salted almonds Ruth noticed the redness of Teresa's eyes; her cheeks, too, were blotched and swollen.

'Your parents told me about the excursion being cancelled,' she said to Elena, 'so I thought I'd give you an hour or two. I was just about to give you up and walk up to see if José was around.'

'You wouldn't have found him either,' said Elena.

'Oh?'

'No, he's gone,' said Ruth.

Elena was pouring out glasses of sweet muscatel. 'I'm glad you came – we can have some fun. So what's happened with your phone?'

'I'll explain . . . Wait, I've got something to show you.' Teresa went out into the hall and came back taking a sweater out of the bag.

'It's perfect,' Elena said when she had put it on. 'You're a clever girl.' And indeed its watery greens and blues with a thin line of gold went wonderfully with Elena's hair. She was turning in a mirror while Teresa smoothed and tweaked the wool.

Teresa let herself smile. But as Elena went to plump herself down on the bed, thrilled with her present, the shorter woman suddenly froze in the mirror, as if the sight of herself holding the empty bag had taken her by surprise. A hand reached up to her face.

'Why didn't you ring before? Why did you leave it?'

'Oh, Elena – ' she sobbed.

Elena put her arm around her and gently sat her on the bed.

'I only started to get worried yesterday morning,' she explained in a low voice. 'I'd promised to go and visit my parents this week, and we'd arranged that Eduardo would stay in Zaragoza until Easter and then just come over for lunch on Easter day, as he can't stand family occasions – but I wanted to go away. The night before I'd been on duty at the clinic so I could get the first train to Caspe – my father was going to meet me at the station . . .'

She was winding a damp handkerchief round her hand, as if bandaging a cut.

'I got up at six to catch the train. Eduardo was asleep – I left a note. Then – you know how it is – sometimes you have a premonition – recently he'd been getting these phone calls late at night. They never lasted more than a few minutes, and afterwards he was always closed up and didn't want to talk. And when I asked him he'd snap at me, "I'd tell you if it were important". You know how stubborn he is.' This to Elena, who lit a cigarette.

Ruth asked, 'So you went back from the station?'

'No. I telephoned him while I was waiting for the train. The phone was engaged. So I rang my parents and told them I'd be getting a later train –'

'You rang them? At six?'

'They're farmers. I went back to the flat, and as I came into the hall there was this smell of smoke. And my first thought was there'd been some disaster – perhaps he'd gone out leaving the gas on, so I rushed into the kitchen and there he was, quite white, covered in sweat with a burning curl of paper in his hands – a letter, it looked like. So I said, "Man, what are you doing?" And then – I couldn't help it, I was a bit hysterical, I suppose – anyway, I began to laugh, and I made some joke about him making breakfast, and usually he'd have laughed too, but this time he began to shout –'

'What sort of things?'

'Oh to leave him alone, not to interfere in things which I had nothing to do with. I was so angry I didn't argue or shout back as I ought to have done but just walked out of the building. I spent last night at my parents'.'

'You haven't spoken to him since then?'

'I've phoned, but as Elena says, it's always engaged.'

Elena said gently, 'Perhaps we should tell the police?'

'I did think about it. I'm so worried he might do something stupid – you remember that business at Atocha station, but about a month ago he told me – I know perhaps I ought not to pay attention to it, for his own good – he said that if ever he were absent for a few days without telling me where he was going I was not to worry and above all not in any circumstances to tell the police. He was quite adamant.'

Elena said under her breath, 'How long is Eduardo going to go on living in the past?'

They fell silent; distantly a church clock struck the hour. There was a sizzle as Elena lit a second cigarette. Perhaps it was the flicker of the flame – she had had to scrape the little paper squib several times against the battered emery – or a movement of Teresa's, pushing back a spot-light towards the rug on the wall so that the glare had gone and a dim warm light came to take their place, but the sense of superfluousness Ruth had felt when the others were trying on the sweater had gone: the questions she had asked had made her one of them.

Elena spoke almost to herself: 'Why was he burning that paper?'

Teresa shrugged miserably. 'I don't know. Recently he has been away almost every weekend – he told me there was something on his mind, something he needed to settle. It's just like two years ago, when –'

The clamour of the telephone made them jump. Elena picked up the phone eagerly, but as she listened she mouthed the word: Pedro. She nodded. 'Listen, my cousin's here. And Ruth. I'll ask them, but I don't think . . .' She cupped her hand over the receiver, saying, 'He wants to know if we'd like to go up to the drums in Calanda on Friday night.'

The others looked bemused.

'Listen, we can't talk now. Let me give you a ring some time.' Then she said to Ruth, 'He wants to speak to you.'

The voice was brutal but reassuring.

'Well, have you smashed up my car?'

'Not yet. Give me just a bit longer.' She tried not to seem too eager as she asked, 'You haven't seen anything of José, have you?'

'No. I thought you said –'

'He wasn't up there, so I came back.'

51

'Yes, I saw the car. Listen, about the drums –' His persistence made her glad.

'It's as Elena says. We'll give you a ring.'

'All right.'

When the phone was down, something made her want to go back.

'Stay to supper – there's enough.'

'No, really. I've still got –'

Elena offered to give her a lift.

'No, no. It's air I need. I promise to ring if José comes back.'

She felt the brush of their cheeks. As she walked up through the orchard the old nectarines creaked like a ship hove to against the wind.

7

Passing the civil guard barracks on her way up into the town, with its ambiguous inscription 'Everything for the Fatherland', Ruth considered Teresa's unwillingness to talk to the police. When she had visited the barracks shortly after her arrival in Spain to ask about a visa a young guard behind the desk had filed his fingernails meticulously throughout the exchange, a brass crucifix standing on the desk; his attitude had brought home to her the real danger of a right-wing coup d'état. It had reminded her that military coups, such as the one mounted by General Franco in 1936, were a feature of Spanish history, for the army tended to think of itself as the people's last resort.

The streets were wet. As she took the steep short-cut up from the Avenida de Aragón she heard the barking of tethered dogs on outlying farms; through a barred window the faces of a family flickered before a television set. A cat with a skinned tail mewed at her before skulking away on to a building site, the fine bone scraping – it must have been mutilated by schoolboys. In an alley she heard the sound of two drums behind a garage door; the stutter stopped and she heard a low voice giving instructions: she imagined a father teaching his son in preparation for Good Friday.

A flight of steps led up to Plaza Mendizábal beside the front of a church. The door on to the porch was open and she entered, realising that she'd never been inside before: it pleased her that such a small town still had secrets. Like the great Santa María on the *plaza*, the interior was as clear as that of a reformed church: she fended off the images of desecration which began to crowd her, of the anarchists purple and black flag, of men urinating on the altar, of the bonfire of church furniture in the street outside. A single bulb divided the part of the place in which she was from the darkness ahead: a lingering trace of incense suggested that Mass had been said there that day. She moved instinctively towards the light.

Ever since her childhood she had loved most in Catholic churches the arrays of candles, those wavering fields of warmth and colour. A shaft of pain, as she stepped forwards, took her breath away, but she withstood it, entranced by the ripple of the flames and the faint honey-scent of the wax. Behind the candles stood a statue draped in purple so that she could only guess at the glass tears, the set expression of compassion.

She could not pray, but finding a five-duro piece in her pocket dropped it into the slot marked 'Alms'; it landed on wood. Taking a candle she fitted it on to a spike in the iron tray and, aware of a welling in her eyes, bit her lip. She knew how far, if she let herself, she could go down the path of repose in the notion of God, with its promise of grace and encouragement to render the self up to an invisible whole. It would have ashamed her to admit this to José, for whom the integrity of the church had been tainted by its support for the dictatorship – though he would have admitted it had become more critical towards the end. It ashamed her, too, a little; but now . . . The warmth of the candles was about equal to the seep of the morning sun through a linen counterpane.

Suddenly her mind focused on two voices whose soft urgency had the tone of the confessional; now a chair-leg squealed and two men emerged from a side door with a tattoo of footsteps, a cough, a chink of keys. Hearing the ceremony of goodbyes, she recognised one of the men as the young curate who assisted the parish priest of Santa María; he coughed again, his fist to his mouth. The second man remained in darkness for a moment before emerging; at the sight of him Ruth's instinct drove her back, too, into the shadows.

He strode past.

'Eduardo!'

'¿Qué?' His jump was terrifying; she was frightened less by him than by his fear. It frightened her too that on seeing her he controlled this at once, swiftly taking her in while she measured the change in his features.

José's cousin was a well-built man in his forties, with a body over-weight from lack of physical exercise. His hair and moustache were the colour of dead embers, and the moustache drooped, lending him an almost comic seriousness: its slight movement could promise, or conceal, a smile. The skin around the eyes creased with an irony so habitual as to make one uneasy; now the lines on his face were engraved with darkness and the moustache was two black brush-strokes on the skin.

'Eduardo! It's me, Ruth – José's . . . Listen, your wife is here. She and Elena – they're so worried – Listen . . .'

The last word was uttered with shock, for the man she thought she knew – the one who teased her for her Englishness – had turned away and was already half out of the church. But it was the expression on the face of the curate as he watched the door creak to, its concern and bafflement, that unsettled her.

'Can I be of any assistance?'

The curate was beside her, his face composed again, repressing another cough. She was tempted by the offer, though she did not know if it was the young man's extreme handsomeness or the idea of unburdening her troubles on to a neutral listener which attracted her. It was not the first time she had felt the appeal of the confession box, its anonymity and fixed method of relief. Besides, didn't she have more than enough to confess? But she was not of his Church, and Eduardo's behaviour troubled her. Thanking the curate hurri-edly, she came out just in time to see the solid figure of José's cousin hesitate at the top of the street, his shabby anorak grey under a street-lamp as he turned and vanished.

As she came up the steps into the small square she halted for a second on the paved area beside the fountain. The sight of Eduardo a moment before had induced a wave of loneliness; now that was replaced by an intense curiosity. For in a gap at the top of one of the roller-blinds of the flat's living-room – a blind lowered swiftly so that the strats were not as dense at the top as at the bottom – a thread of light hung on the dark like the tuning pin of an old-fashioned wireless.

PART TWO

THE CHAPEL IN THE HILLS

8

Ruth had mounted the dank staircase, and finding the bunch of keys in her pocket inserted one into the lock as if it were glass.

'José?'

'I'm here.'

A hollow clicking led her down the hall past the open door of his bedroom to where he was standing in the larder trying to relight the gas pilot.

'Damn thing's gone out again,' he growled. 'It's the wind.'

She could hear a certain constriction in his voice, as if her own embarrassment were infecting him.

'It was working earlier – I had a bath. Use these.' She took out a book of matches she had been given in a restaurant in the south and gave it to him. When the blue flame had budded and bloomed he returned the matches and just looked at her, so that she was suddenly conscious of the mess of her untrimmed hair, and reached up to it. His face had its El Greco gauntness: his mood was deep *sombra*. Yet relief flooded over her, and she was dragged forwards into the spill of his eyes, to kiss him, smooth his harsh hair.

But he remained still, so it was like kissing an icon, and in the end she pulled away.

In the kitchen they sat on either side of the table and it seemed to her that to watch him peel an orange – his thumb forcing the thick skin off – was, for the time being, enough. The sight of his elegant face coming undone as he chewed the segments almost made her laugh with relief; somehow she was reminded of the sign *'Histórica y Heróica'* outside the town. Sitting there in silence, breathing in the mundane familiarity of the scene, she felt the absurdity of having made such a violent interior drama out of her need for him when that need could be met – or almost – by his simple presence. Now he was there she wanted to tell him about her journey, but she supposed what had happened must be obvious from her premature return.

The wind was rattling the blinds and, in a lull, she thought she could make out the dialogue of drums behind the garage door.

'I've just seen something strange. Eduardo –'

'You've seen him?'

'Yes – in the little church below here. He was with the new curate. I tried to speak to him, but he just ignored me. And the odd thing is Teresa –'

'You've seen her too? Where?'

'Down at the school. I met your sister at the house in Belmonte. Pedro lent me a car. Then, when we got back here, she was waiting –' Her voice trembled. 'Oh José – you've no idea how glad I am to see you –'

'What's she doing here?'

'Teresa? She's worried about Eduardo. Something about some phone calls. She found him burning a letter.'

'Isn't Elena –?'

'The school trip was cancelled because of the weather. You should have seen the floods outside Valencia –'

'I suppose Teresa's told the police?'

'No – Eduardo told her not to. But don't you think we should?'

He shook his head firmly.

'Why not?'

'Because it's his problem. If only I knew. But I was doing some painting up at Belmonte – as you knew – when he drove up . . .' His voice had risen: she could tell that in the silence of the night he had been eager to explain; now the well dried: either he had remembered her journey and wanted to mark the rift it had caused, or there was something else . . .

'We ought to let Teresa know he's here. She's terrified.'

He swallowed – a reflex of the Adam's apple; it had been the same when she had kissed him. For a while he had been looking down; now he glanced at her and she seemed to detect a sheepishness, as if he were remembering something she had once blurted out to him in a moment of frustration at the *machista* assumptions his good will was not enough to eradicate: 'I'm your equal, José – you must tell me more. I expect to know what's happening . . .', so that his next speech was like a concession.

'My cousin's in trouble. I don't know what trouble exactly, because he's forbidden me to press him. There were a couple of things he had to do in Alcañiz – and then . . . He's coming back here soon, and I expect he'll want to talk to me alone.'

His last word wandered on the air. He had finished the orange some time before and the peel lay on the plate like broken china.

'Well, I imagine you'll be tired from your journey?'

In the repressed silence which followed she seemed to see the figure of Eduardo turn and vanish again at the top of the street, and she suffered again the rejection she had felt that night up at the refuge beneath the stars. That had been the first sign that Eduardo might come between her and José, that he could prove to be another of the prohibitions to her absorption into José's world, for she had sensed a bond between the two men which both united and kept them apart.

Why did she feel that sense of separation again now? It wasn't only José's slightly awkward admission to her; something about his earlier part in their conversation, his eagerness to press her on certain matters, his lack of interest in others – made her sure he knew more. She would have liked to ask him about it, but she felt that by going south she had renounced her right to do so. There could be no right of appeal, for she judged herself guilty.

'Will you speak to Teresa, then?'

'All right.'

She nodded. 'Listen, I've got something of yours . . .'

They met again at the door of his bedroom and she handed him his brother's book which she had found up at the house in Belmonte, her letter breaking the pages. As he took it, she felt as if she had acknowledged his right to reject her.

An icon kiss. And Ruth gritted her teeth to enter her cold room.

She lay for a long time on the made bed without taking off her shoes.

She supposed she ought to have felt relieved that something had come to distract José from her transgression, like a soldier secretly welcoming the bad weather which delays an advance. One day, at least, she knew he must let her tell him about the journey – the hardest thing was not being able to talk about it now. There was only one person she could speak to about such things, and she had made him the last. She promised herself that if he should let her she would relate what had happened completely straight, though like the letter she had sent it would be another case of honesty not being enough.

She knew that neither of them would be taken in if she were, with hindsight, to present the failure of her journey as a pretext for having made it. In going to Granada she had hoped to change everything; not to give up her work – although even that had crossed her mind, but to make plans for a future which would involve Tom, and which would reveal her time in Teruel for what she had always felt it to be: a period of research. Perhaps it was inevitable that the absence of any criticism from José made her harder on herself: she began to regret ever having come to Spain; at the same time she felt a violent need for comfort – the warmth of his body beside hers.

Turning on to her back she saw in the circle from the bedside lamp a long crack in the ceiling plaster; in places where the surface had actually flaked off there were irregular cavities. They seemed to her now like a map of the waterways in the region: the tiny rushing streams which began secretly, rustling out from beneath bracken in the high sierra to swell the deep, motionless reservoirs in the valleys. She remembered standing on a bank of pebbles that morning by the Guadalope, loving the lacquered stones at her feet, and, earlier that

day, leaning on the bridge beneath which the water dashed before its
meandering descent to the broad valley of the Ebro. Now Manrique's
lines came back to her:

> 'Our lives are the rivers
> Which will flow into the sea
> Which is death . . .'

She remembered her first train journey into the province, when
she had called unannounced on José during a university vacation:
she had sent the postcard telling him of her intention to visit him far
too late. This was because her whole idea of the journey – or at least
the idea she thought she had – was to drift from place to place as the
mood took her; she had some idea that growing up was to do with
developing a sense of resignation to the slow passage of time – a result
of seeing several 'road movies'; in fact, this was a pose, for she had
one of José's letters crushed into the inside pocket of her jacket and an
image, too, of his face among the smudge of drums and rain.

The train pulled up at Caspe station one afternoon. Alone on the
platform, except for the station-master in his blue jacket casually
ringing a brass bell, she felt the caress of a wind hard as linen on her
face. As the sleek train oozed away it revealed a completely gutted
church on the far side of the tracks, its rows of arched windows fram-
ing a measureless sky.

The airless ticket-office, with the trains chalked on a green board
and one sleeping soldier lying with his bedding roll under his head,
was like a frontier between two worlds: they had told her in Zaragoza
that the trains extended no further south.

As she walked up into the deserted town at siesta time she felt she
understood why. It seemed drained of life; a De Chirico geometry of
shadows and concrete flats where the dry breeze disturbed circus
posters on the walls and softly combed the fields of wheat beyond the
remnants of the place. Her parents had made her promise not to
hitch-hike and yet there was no other way to get to the next town of
Alcañiz, unless she were to wait for the bus the next morning . . .
Alone and without transport she had realised she was no drifter,

willing to sit out the film of her life until a deeper understanding should present itself. To linger in Caspe bored and slightly frightened her; she felt that unless she kept moving the loneliness at her back would catch up in the silence of a hostel bedroom, the fly-blown squalor of the station bar. She asked the barman if any of his clients were driving to Alcañiz; after a brief discussion one man agreed to take her when he'd finished his beer.

Chewing a stale *bocadillo* at the bar, she tried to disentangle, from the rough quarrying of rural voices above the television, some phrase – or even a word – which two years of a Spanish degree would enable her to understand. Their voices were baked like the earth; the face of the man who had offered to take her creased like a leather shoe so that his age was difficult to judge. As they drove out of Caspe she tried to assume an experienced air while the plastic oil drums bumped against her rucksack in the back of the van. She realised it was not just a matter of a thick accent but one of intonation, for she could not at first work out from what the driver was saying whether he was friendly, or giving her instructions, or even angry; finally she understood one phrase, which gladdened her: 'I could see right away you wasn't the usual sort of tourist.' She was alarmed to see the van tumbling off the road into a field of wheat, but the driver got out and a minute later she herself stepped out into the blazing sun, which the chaff tossed up by a noisy harvester connected to the earth with a river of gold. She helped the labourers hold bags open as the grain poured into them from a great chute. Their rough voices rose over the racket of the machine and a veil of midges prickled her face and arms.

She took an immediate dislike to Alcañiz because she was trapped there: as at Caspe there was only one bus, in the early morning. Besides, in the sun-blanched desolation of the streets up to the square a couple of overweight boys, one of whom had shouted an obscenity as she emerged from the shadows of the bus station, followed at her heels; later from her balcony she would see them waiting for her below. In the declining rays of sun the awkwardly shaped *plaza* had the tattered air of an old ochre-painted setting for a Spanish operetta, overladen with a cats-cradle of loudspeaker and telegraph wires. Speaking to José's grandmother from the telephone under the arcade she said that she would call again the next day, for it was part of her journey's self-induced romance to maintain the pretence of independence. But of course when she did speak to him the next morning from another village he insisted on coming to meet her. And so it was at an anonymous crossroads in a place whose name was familiar from some history book that she saw the grey van back up and felt the brush of his lips. And then they were seated beneath the creaking awning of the Bar Imperial, speaking diffidently, for her Spanish came in fits and starts, of very little – of how his father still used this van for transporting peaches but he was going to let him have it, of how Elena had got a teaching job in Alcañiz, of their first meeting at the drums.

The four or five days she spent in the house in Belmonte seemed to swim past with the steady progress of a dream which was more real than life itself. In the electric peace of the country, time moved with a deeper rhythm, one which was closer to the rhythms of the body. She did not think that she had ever slept so deeply – or that, waking, she had been more alive to physical sensations: the crispness of bleached sheets, the sharpness of stones beneath her shoes, the thick wine they bought in the village shop with its smell of cured hams and seasoned olives and slabs of quince jelly. One evening she stepped out on to the terrace and saw the whole valley etched in moonlight, the almond and peach trees exactly still, the ruin on the crags behind a single decayed tooth against the night, and it felt as if a door had opened in her body and that the landscape had come to dwell inside her like a child. In the penumbra of those interconnected rooms with their beamed ceilings painted with iris and red curtains concealing stuffy alcoves she and José would meet, it seemed, by chance. The silence of their limping conversations was occupied by the house's history which sometimes came to sit with them at the table in the form of children in fancy dress. These had begun to appear one morning when, on entering the oval dining-room with its linen-shrouded chandelier, Ruth had realised that she was being watched by a little boy in the costume of a Velázquez duke; after that she couldn't emerge on to the dusty stairs without seeing a tiny sailor-girl run down them after a hoop or glimpsing a boy in the white cloak and tas-selled fez of a Moroccan legionary. Later José told her that he and his sister had once played such games.

He also had a motorbike at that time and she clung on as they wound down on to the plain and up again into Alcañiz, up the preci-pitous street leading to the Plaza de España. In the dust of a window-less room on to the square she saw a flame burst, lighting first his arm, then his long face, mahogany eyes. At once the match went out, leaving a whiff of smoke and, beneath it, the cologne he wore which barely concealed the fragrance of sweat.

'Wait,' he murmured. A second flame. And then she took the match as his hand rummaged in a chest, bringing out books so that, by the light of the flame, she could see the title pages of works by Unamuno and Joaquín Costa and the official stamp of the republic.

'This town hasn't had a library for over forty years,' he said.

And Ruth bit her lip, feeling the sheer weight of the dictatorship.

That evening they walked up towards the castle above the village. She saw it in a crevice in the rock – so black it might have been a hole, except it was too perfect in shape: a tiny coin among the clumps of thyme and camomile. At first she thought it was a peseta, as eroded by wind and rain as the hills around, but it weighed even less, and there was no head of Franco on the back or the legend 'Francisco Franco: by the Grace of God, Ruler of Spain'.

José's voice, half drowned by the racket of crickets, explained, because it was his history, 'It's an anarchist voucher. I've got a drawer full of them at home. When they were here in the first year of the war they collectivised Belmonte, distributing an equal number of those to each villager to buy oil, salt, black bread. When the com-munists took over they nationalised the collectives.'

The coin lay on her desk during her final examinations in England. As time passed, she had come to think of Belmonte as the embodiment of the Spanish version of 'To call a spade a spade': 'To call bread, bread, and wine, wine.' In those days returning to Teruel was one option among many – so many lives presented themselves, impossible because unknown. She would have liked to do something with Tom, but he was remote and irresolute; there was an element of vindictiveness, too, in the notion of going to a place they had not discovered together.

It surprised her when her tutor took her idea seriously, as it was a historical subject, and beneath it lay the memory of José. His dark voice; his inner calm. The fact that he had never touched her – that made her curious. Letters were exchanged, and calls – news of his job at the library, and suddenly there they were, two strangers in a bare flat with the hot night outside, moths flattened like pancakes on the windows.

She loved it because it was her doing – her family and friends were full of admiration, yet secretly it was easy because it involved only her. It was her secret, too, that the only hard thing was coping with boredom. Little happened in the small town and what did – the opening of the library, the film club José started, the sculpture exhibition – was less interesting in itself than in the way it affected people who for years had had only the disco, an annual car race, the occasional folk-music demonstration in the old theatre – and, of course, the drums.

In the autumn they kissed for the first time, something which excited her and made her happy, for of course the chance of it had underlain their friendship; yet it also set off a train of doubts and questions which would lend it the fascination of the forbidden. For the memory of Tom, the intensity of their feelings and the promises they had made each other, danced behind her like a shadow, ensuring that whatever happened with José remained unresolved. She began to feel as she once had when, after recklessly throwing away some notes towards her thesis, she had been forced to ransack her waste-paper basket, convinced that among them was an observation which would provide the key to her whole argument. And – there was anyway little else to do in the hours after her day's work – she took to taking long walks, as if hoping to find some clue to her failure in the country beyond the town.

Alcañiz lay in a moon landscape whose crested hills were all that remained after years of erosion and subsidence. Like Sancho Panza's governorship, it was an island surrounded by land, except that it was several islands moored to an abrupt hill on which stood the castle, four-square and barracks-like, a tumbledown chapel in its back yard. The church of Santa María dominated the lower section of the place, with its two narrow towers on either side of a wavy-topped façade, a blue-and-green-tiled cupola behind. From a distance these two buildings, castle and church, seemed to be man-made versions of the hills which rose out of the plain like the supports of a house from which the walls had been blown away. And Alcañiz itself, a jumble of new flats and terracotta roofs, was the scale of a model on the floor of that ruined palace of the winds.

That was what Ruth knew her friends in England could not imagine – the sense of space when she gazed down at the town scattered on its two hills, the bullring a magic circle of lights above the darkening river. Nor could they see the changes the seasons wrought in the earth, disclosing secret places and consuming others like the huge cloud-shadows which fled across the porous hills.

The heat fell like a curse, rendering sovereignty of the land to the bloodless or cold-fleshed; snakes writhed on the melting roads and the death-rattle of cicadas sent an alternating current through the silver trunks of olive trees. Now wheat stalks were brittle, motionless in white light, and shade slapped the cheeks, leaving you panting for breath, head throbbing with the after-images of crags and trees. The sun was a dark comet shrivelling the world's crust, while what water there was rotted at the bottom of basins awaiting its execution by the guillotines which regulated its flow to the edges of orchards. There was no choice but to siesta; in the hushed flat sleep closed shutters, bringing dreams of the dead railway, its track a cauterised wound across the red land, faded butterflies dancing above the rubble of its station buildings. Or Ruth would wake with the image of a southern street, and almost smell the stench of drains trapped by its canvas awning.

Then, gradually, the heat began to ease. In the second olive harvest she saw one of the canvases olives were tossed on to after picking strung up on a wall to dry, a great circular oil-stain on it like the declining sun. The aspens and birches by the river were bronze, and the shots of huntsmen volleyed in the cliffs. When, driving back from one of her interviews, she parked the van in an unknown village, the luminous sky would endow everything she saw – the biscuit houses, a mulberry tree growing out of the crumbling tower of the church, the greyhound-like mongrels chasing each other perpetually through the streets, their nails clicking on the stones – with the vividness of a child's painting. Sometimes she would go no further than the terrace above Alcañiz, where, at the hour of the *paseo,* people came out to chat and show off their extravagantly dressed children in a flurry of church bells and the discarded husks of sunflower seeds. And the plane trees by the river would fragment and chase themselves across the sky in a metallic twitter of starlings.

At this season she was afflicted with images of earlier wars, perhaps because the copper light suggested to her the red coats of the English soldiers when they met the French on the battlefield outside Alcañiz. Or perhaps it was because it gave the hills and villages the sepia quality of engravings in the books of nineteenth-century travellers in the peninsula such as Borrow or Mérimée. Then, in the last rays of the sun, the ruined walls of a castle would swarm with Carlist soldiers, their skull and crossbones fluttering above the town while musket-fire chipped the rocks at her feet. As night fell she would imagine oil lamps shining in the *miradores* of the 'good' part of the town, and the glow of coal in braziers beneath round tables under whose long cloths the women of a family would extend their feet while the men emerged, loud, frock-coated and a little tipsy, from the gateway of the gentlemen's club. In November the white smoke of bonfires rose among the branches of persimmon trees, hiding their flame-orange fruits. And on the moonlit path up to a hermitage the horns of a dead yew stirred suddenly, causing her heart to falter as she stood beneath a cold outpouring of stars.

When she returned from England after Christmas – no longer determined to suffer, she had learned that a taxi from Caspe was actually cheap – snow still dusted the tilled earth, turning bare almond trees charred black beneath a lowering sky; on the corners of streets bulbs in glazed niches glowed fitfully above plaster saints and the light from a farm door would fall across steaming dung heaps and piles of maize. Then Teruel was a land of Goyesque shadows, and at a night fiesta in one of the villages a vast bonfire rose to the height of the buildings in the square. Its heat was so fierce that the owners of a house with a wooden porch had to paint the lintel with water to prevent it catching fire. And a man suddenly executed a strange dance, raising his arms like antlers as he twisted at the edge of the flames.

In January came a dazzle of high blue which made the pasture on the passes of the sierra precious as silk. They played tennis down by the brimming river in whose banks shoots of wild asparagus broke through the stiff mud and narcissi fluttered in the chill air. Then larks soared and tumbled and the flicker of a wagtail skimmed the green wheat. Already the great stockades of poplars along the river sported mists of flags, their dry rustle echoing the stream. And loveliest of all, the blossom was out, so that driving eastwards in the van the road would wind through silver olives as clouds of almond petals scattered on the gold-white earth.

But it was on a wet morning in spring, when she had taken a letter from Tom out into the country to re-read, that what she thought of as the land's secret was revealed to her. Ruth had been troubled before – she had noticed this when trying to describe it to her friends – by the landscape's fragmentary quality, the incompleteness which made its streets and the spaces they led out to like the jottings in an artist's sketchbook. It was as if the eroded barren hills extended into the

town's buildings and paving stones, so that even there you had the
sense that you were living with just enough. Sitting on a bench outside the hermitage of Santa Barbara on its high outcrop, looking back
at the town whose church bell was monotonously striking, it
occurred to her that the landscape was an equation in which an element was always missing. Just as it seemed about to arrive at fullness
something withdrew; it was Nature's version of Purgatory. Unlike
the permanent green of England with its gradual inflexions of fertility, here each season replaced one absence with another, patching
and repatching like the peeling bark of a plane tree. When the wheat
swirled on the plain the hills were bone-dry, and when it rained for
days only the cypresses grew darker against the earth. And, looking
back at the town, she saw the similarity with her relationship with
José. Like the wine at the bottom of a glass it circled about a lack
which kept it in motion, for it maintained in them both a measure of
curiosity.

Tom's letter had a Spanish stamp on it. She did not know if it had
been in England at Christmas or earlier that the idea of coming to
Spain himself had crossed his mind. It wasn't until a few months
before that she had received a postcard from Burgos by which she
could begin to map his progress as he travelled south, bypassing
Teruel. José knew about the letters: she was honest; he appeared
unshaken when she asked him that evening if they could go out
somewhere for a drive – she had something she wanted to speak to
him about.

He had driven them, rain pummelling the roof, down the chute of
the Calle Mayor out into open country, drops flickering in the van's
headlamps. The road twisted past the reservoir; she remembered the
village under its surface, but not its name. The rain dripped from
almond trees, each a dark individual above the pitch of the earth. An
unknown road running beside a ploughed field under black, bone-
shaped hills. They came to a village with a deep gorge at its heart.
Getting out of the van and hurrying across the bridge under José's
umbrella, they took refuge in a bar which clung on over the lichen-

covered, ivy-entangled cleft. Alone in there, except for a flea-bitten sheep-dog in a basket running in her sleep, and a boy listening to a transistor radio, they had the conversation in which she stated to him, finally, her decision to go south.

'It'll only be for a fortnight.'

'Well, you must go,' he said.

They went out into the night and, as they crossed the bridge, she had looked down and seen an infinitely long, thin, white streak of water plunging down beneath her between tall rocks into utter darkness.

9

The squeal of a chair leg. The clock read something past three – so she must have been asleep; an itch of saliva on her cheek meant she had slept with her mouth open. It was there again – the scrape of wood on tile, and then a low murmur which might have been coming from the street. The room was black; it must still be profound night.

She needed to relieve herself; perhaps, too, her tampon would need to be changed? She put a sweater over her shoulders, her toes into slippers – they were like a human hand caressing her feet. Then she crossed the passage.

Immediately she opened the door of her room the hubbub stopped: two voices had been speaking in the living-room. A faint whiff of black tobacco clung to the damp air, and there was another smell, too – the sweet cloying scent of brandy.

Her face was pale in the bathroom mirrors – even her nightshirt was a warmer tone. José's leather washbag stood, now, on the shelf beside hers; there was his electric razor next to a packet of Cafeaspirina. Water churned cantankerously. On the way back to her bedroom she hesitated in the kitchen doorway; the voices had dropped again, but through the food hatch she thought she saw the waver of a candle. They were waiting, she realised, for her to return to her room.

'José,' she said.

The door opened and he appeared, a tall bulk in the hallway.

'Eduardo's here. We're talking. You can't sleep?'

She shook her head.

'Is he all right?'

'Ruth – I did say. Tomorrow. Please. It would be best . . .'

'Holá, inglesa.'

She saw him seated beyond José, beyond the candle; his pale face flushed with drink, his eyes glistening in the shadows of sleeplessness. His mouth, wavering beneath the moustache, conveyed sadness through the smile meant for her; one arm propped beneath his chin, he looked like a figure in one of those religious pictures in Spanish churches whose yellow faces are so dim behind the varnish that it is hard to tell whether the effect is deliberate or the result of years of candle-soot. His hand shook as he retrieved his cigarette from the full ash-tray.

There was a bottle of Carlos III on the table; Ruth could smell it on José's breath. Was Eduardo drinking again? His torn grey anorak over a chair back was like a third drinker at the table.

He went on, 'Thanks for being concerned about me.'

'You know, your wife –'

José said, 'He knows.'

'It'll be sorted out very soon . . . Don't worry, English girl.' As he said this Eduardo leaned back on the chair and stretched, his huge yawn displaying a crop of neglected teeth. The movement of his abdomen inside the home-made sweater revealed a much larger body than José's; he had put on weight since their trip up to the mountains. He picked up a glass and with a barely suppressed belch swirled the liquid briefly before taking a sip. In her nightshirt, in front of these two – the man in the doorway, the older one beyond the candle, Ruth felt suddenly self-conscious, like a child disturbing her parents' dinner party on the pretext of needing a glass of water.

She peered at José's face to see if he were drunk, but he seemed sober enough.

'I'll explain everything tomorrow,' he said. 'But now . . .'

'It's all right. I'm going back to bed. I'll just make myself some tea to help me sleep. You don't want anything?'

'No.'

Unexpectedly, José had taken her hand. She kissed him on his rough cheek, whispering, 'Good night.' Then the door had closed, a chair squeaked, and she knew that the two men were waiting for her to return to her room. But soon they would be murmuring again across the candle flame – two foreigners with foreign troubles, a foreign history.

She moved fast, for her excuse was a brief one; she did not think they had heard her return to her bedroom where she removed the used cassette from the recorder and reversed a blank one with a soft clatter into the aperture. By the time she was back in the kitchen the monkey-chatter of water on the gas had increased enough to conceal the rest of her actions – the placing of the tape-recorder behind the half-open door of the food hatch in such a way that it was concealed by a jug of dried lavender. The record lever had the stiffness of the piano keys in the house in Belmonte.

In her bedroom she placed the glass of tea on her desk and, with a sudden need to appear busy to herself, opened a book at random – it was the exercise book she kept for noting down her recordings. She read the last entries:

> Calanda – 8 February – Pilar Ferrer Ruiz (84 years) – 90 minutes. Redistribution of Property – Civil Marriages. Mas de las Matas – 10 February – Fernando Pacheco (73 years) – 25 minutes. Reprisals of August 1936. Execution of Suspected Rightists. Death of Padre Ariño,

smiling nervously to herself at the thought of indexing José and Eduardo in the same way. Dropping the book as if it burned she heard again the low voices in the other room, and the excitement and guilt at what she was doing caused her to stand and pace for a few moments. She knew she should return to the kitchen and stop the tape immediately; at the same time she was afraid of being given away in forty minutes' time by the discreet click which, when she was interviewing, made her feel like the Cinderella of postgraduate studies.

She lay on the bed to think. It was paradoxical that the fact of once having behaved badly towards José made it easier to do so again. She told herself to get up and go to the kitchen, but already five minutes had gone and it seemed too late now to prevent the crime. Besides, that would turn it into a half-crime, a failure on its own terms.

Finally tiring of these conundrums, she must have drifted into sleep, for the next thing she was aware of was a faint aura of light in the room. Suddenly wide awake she heard the creak of a door, whispering voices, the shuffle of feet in the corridor outside. From the crack beneath her bedroom door came a sudden blast of air: the front door had been opened. Then she heard the double ratchet of the lock and the sound of feet on the stairs.

She supposed that this must be dawn – this change in the quality of rain to include light, as if a few drops of grey had been injected into the inky solution. The white Seat had got lost already on a twist in the road, which rose rapidly on this side of the town almost to the height of the castle before ribboning down and then up into the sierra. She glimpsed the spill of its headlights, far ahead, in a breach in the grey rosettes of the olive trees floating on the mist. Anyway she did not want to come upon the parked car suddenly on a bend and risk being recognised; at a distance, and among the charcoal hills, she did not think they would give much attention to the pair of headlights nicking the mist almost a kilometre behind them.

She told herself she had been lucky. It had been a matter of throwing on what clothes she could – there had been no time even to wash, as she had seen, on hoisting a blind, the two men, one carrying a full duffle-bag, crossing the square. An impulse – one which turned out not to be mistaken – made her choose the road towards the hills. Yet she did not think she would have caught up with them if, while she was waiting for a pair of traffic lights beside the hospital, she had not seen Eduardo's car appear suddenly from the Avenida de Aragón and turn left in front of her on to the main road. She had held her breath –

surely they had seen her? But – perhaps because they did not know the car – they had passed without a look; as she waited, ignoring the green light now, she realised that they must have made a detour down to the all-night petrol station on the Zaragoza road, where the fruit lorries refuelled on their way north.

She took the cassette-player out of her shoulder-bag and rested it on the seat beside her. As soon as she was up she had gone into the kitchen to see if either of the two men had discovered the machine. Now it seemed likely that her plan had worked and she had got the thing beside her she again felt guilty for having deceived them. Perhaps by destroying the tape – or just by not listening to it – she could short-circuit her remorse? Surely the crime would be in using the recording, not in having made it?

There was a click; the machine had ceased winding back. Still Ruth hesitated, until the desire to know – and the ease of the action – forced her hand. She reached across to depress the key.

A noise like a shout – she had to turn down the volume swiftly until it resolved into a blur. Perhaps their conversation would be inaudible, thus making her scruples redundant? For a long time there was nothing and she began to think it had not worked – the hatch door had not been open enough or they had moved away from the table to the divan and armchair. Then, above the noise of the car, through a fog of white sound which was like the surface-crackle of an old record, she heard the voices. At first she was baffled by other sounds which, louder than the men, often blocked them out – the slurp of drinking? A chair creaking? The rasp of breath? It took her time, too, to distinguish two strands of conversation – the low, persistent murmur of José; Eduardo's slurred growl of response.

> José: So how long do you think you'll have to be up there?
> Eduardo: Man, I don't know. At least a week, I reckon. Of course I'll get in touch with Tere. Get her to let me know if there's been trouble.

José: Don't you think she might be in danger?

Eduardo: At your sister's? No. I thought she was going to her parents', you see.

José: Mm. And when a week's up?

Eduardo: Should be all right. Got to be – with my work and all. I might get someone just to have a look around the flat first – check the mail-box – that stuff.

José: Do you want me to do that?

Eduardo: Why?

José: Why what?

Eduardo: I mean, why are you doing all this, man? Spend a day looking for a priest? Saying you'll come up tomorrow to help me settle when I've said I'll go alone?

José: That's simple. A friend drives up to the house. He tells me he's in trouble – I'm not to ask why. He's my friend, so I do what he asks. That's simple. And if ever I came to you –'

Eduardo: (a grunt)

José: So now, as a friend, I'm telling you we ought to get some kip. For one thing, you've got to sleep off the drink.

The car jerked into a pot-hole in the road. For a moment, Ruth realised with horror, she had been driving without attention, trying to get some sort of foothold on their conversation; she had not expected that her misdemeanour would expose a deeper layer of obscurity. There was more noise now – feet shuffling, the complaint of wicker; she imagined one of them had blown out the candle. Then silence, or the tape's equivalent of it – an uneven hiss, and she had the disquieting sensation that the two of them were with her in the car, listening. Ahead of her the Seat had turned a sharp bend and was below, descending the incline on the valley's far side.

She thought back to the living-room, trying to envisage the silence. Had one of them stretched out on the divan while the other slumped in the armchair? Or had José gone to his room? Discouraged by the long gap, she was just about to reach across to stop the tape when she was checked by the voice of José, this time barely more than a whisper:

> You're sure there's nothing you want to tell me,
> Eduardo? About what's happened, I mean?
> Eduardo: (a grunt) Why ask that?
> José: I don't know – I just wondered. Several times
> recently I've had the feeling there's something you've
> wanted to speak about, but somehow can't. And then this
> morning you said something which struck me. Something
> I don't . . . That's right. After you told me about the
> chapel and how your father had taken you up there for a
> picnic and so on, you said 'I'm on my own now'. It struck
> me, that's all.
> Eduardo: I thought you said it was simple.
> José: All right. But just remember I'm your friend, and
> if you need to talk . . .

A protracted silence. She drove past a ploughed field in which a few
crows were pecking at the foot of a pair of sticks dressed in a blue
jacket and a pair of rubbish bags. Then Eduardo mumbled:

> There is something I want to talk about. But not
> tonight, OK? Maybe tomorrow, if we can get some brandy
> up to the chapel. But maybe never . . .
> José: All right.

They had stopped speaking, though the machine had gone on for
she did not know how long, absorbing the gulf between them. Ruth
wondered if it would be worth winding on to see if, some time later, it
had caught their departure, but she felt that she had enough to think
about with what had been and not been said.

She switched the machine off – switched off the headlights too, for
it was getting brighter outside. For some time she had been aware of
the lights of a third vehicle following some way behind – at about the
same distance, probably, as her own car was from Eduardo's. The
road turned and bent back on itself continually among terraced

groves, so that the glimmer of the two lights behind would vanish for a long interval before their beams would once again sweep an embankment. The lamps were high: they must belong to a van or small lorry. She knew now roughly what her own car must have looked like to José and Eduardo when they had spotted it first. She could imagine them saying to themselves, as she did now: Elena? But it isn't her car. An early farmer? The police? Maintaining considered distances, the three cars beat their way on up into the sierra.

It was the light which made progress, not the cars, although it would never really get light that day: the sky was too firmly overcast, the rain too much in charge of the world. High up, grey wraiths of cloud were passing swiftly on another brightness like a bad paint-match; the only colour in the landscape was the drab green of grass and fennel stalks trembling by the side of the road. Now the lamps of all three cars had been turned off; the mist had vanished; she noticed that she was going faster in order to keep up with the car ahead. For a while her pursuer seemed to have given up, but later, as it entered a hamlet she had already passed through, she saw that the car was an off-white jeep with a spare tyre on the bonnet. Two men were in the high front seats. Were they following her? She tightened her foot on the accelerator. A hitch-hiker – a young man almost completely concealed by a yellow anorak – was standing on an ancient stone bridge over a river. He stepped out a little into the road as she flashed past; she was reminded of Tom. Not today, she thought, seeing the yellow back and arm stretched out as if to prevent the air from falling. The jeep did not stop either.

The road wound up through a forest of mountain pine; on the side towards the hill patches of wet sandy earth had tumbled across it and these glistened in the rain. The shelf-tops of mountain pines shivered and great gobs of rain plummeted from their branches on to the roof of the car with an alarming clatter. Every now and again a triangular sign showed a flaming match crossed out, with the message 'Danger of Fire'. In certain places near the road the groves of trees had been replaced by lines of small conifers planted by the government forestry agency. 'It's the roots,' José had said to her once up at Belmonte; 'it's the roots of trees which hold this land together and prevent the wind and rain eroding it to desert – in a lot of places it's already too late.'

Convinced she had gone wrong she slowed the car and wound down the window to listen for the jeep behind. A small waterfall was chortling behind the trees, drowning even the shimmering of the birds – a distant ancestor, she supposed, of the river which hooked round Alcañiz. A Spanish swear-word came to her lips. A moment's lack of vigilance had done it – the cascades of mud on the road reminding her of what José had said; now she doubted if she would ever again catch up with the two men in this labyrinth of crackling twigs and dripping pine needles.

A track led up to the right; she turned into it and waited for the jeep. Nothing came. But just when she had shifted the car back to the road's edge to make a three-point turn it appeared round the corner and, braking sharply, narrowly avoided a head-on collision with her as she was manoeuvring across the narrow road.

They faced one another through the windscreens: the pale English girl and her two pursuers. The driver of the jeep had a squarish face and was wearing a denim jacket; his companion, who looked older, had a small sticking-plaster over one eye as if a boil had burst . . . Ruth saw no more for her first thought was to get out of their way; she changed into reverse to edge back, then scrunched forwards. Meanwhile the driver of the other vehicle had himself backed slightly into the steep track so that the high wheels of the jeep tilted precariously away from her as she drove past, giving a quick nod of acknowledgment.

She wondered if the two men would continue along this road towards the sierra, and whether she had done the right thing in obeying her instinct to turn back.

10

There was no sign of Eduardo's car at the foot of the cliff; only a waste-land of mud which extended, pale and creamy, on either side of the road before breaking abruptly off above the river-bed. This too was a wide, flat space across which several rivers linked arms between bands of mud and pebbles. The hills on the far side were as worn as the wet cliff-face. There was barely any vegetation anywhere. A single holm-oak clung on, oddly deformed, at a bend in the stream; a few birches and pines dripped in the opening of a narrow niche in the cliff in which there was a huddle of creosoted huts. The whole place was an instance of what José had said about the lack of replanting; yet it was difficult to believe that this area had ever been wooded: it looked as if it had always been a landscape wavering close to a kind of geological vanishing-point, crumbling and subsiding towards departure from itself.

A narrow pinewood stairway hung, cobweb-like, beneath the angle of the cliff. Parked some way off, Ruth tried to retrace the route she had taken in her mind; the strange thing was that she could not remember a single turn-off between here and the fork which had taken her up into the forest. Had she been wrong to turn back? The two men in the jeep didn't seem to think so. She could see the jeep already approaching the far side of the bridge. An awful thought struck her: perhaps it was she who had led the men after Eduardo and José from Alcañiz? All the more reason to warn them if they were here.

Slipping the tape-recorder into her coat pocket, she began to mount the rickety walkway. As she climbed, the planks creaked beneath her; they were slippery and she had to cling to the wooden balustrade to stop herself falling. The rain spat against the wall of rock, making the chalky surface glisten; the sound of the river was refracted by the cliff, so it seemed to be murmuring in sympathy with the groaning wooden structure. The stone on her left, on the side without a balustrade, was covered with names and dates and obscene symbols. At any moment she expected José and Eduardo to appear around the wall of rock; but she reached the highest platform alone and stood by a brick wall in the cliff. From up here she could see a further stretch of the river curving round beyond a low modern bridge: the water was a series of steel sheets set in the grey land.

The jeep's roof-rack was immediately below now; there was no sign of either of the two men getting out. She pushed open a door in the brick wall.

Rows of wooden chairs with kneelers, a painted pair of gates, beyond them an altar and a carved figure on a brass cone; the interior was well-lit, in spite of the fact that the only light was from mesh-covered windows in the wall through which she had come. When she entered she had a primitive sense of security – the fastness of caves, but as she stepped forwards this was replaced by unease: the floor rose and subsided under her feet – a petrified sea – and she feared that at any moment she might be going to smash her head on the ceiling. The air was stagnant with the odours of dankness and stale incense.

It was a chapel, of course: a rough stoup was cut into the wall by the door, and near this hung a framed woodcut of the resident Virgin with edifying stanzas beneath; yet Ruth felt the place's power was inherited, a rechanneling of some atavistic devotion from before Christianity, whose cult image – a black figure on a brass stand – was an obscure symbol of Woman. A baby grew like fungus on her body, and her blurred features, apart from the gold eyes, looked as if they had been formed by an infinitesimal oozing of water – perhaps she had been shaped from a stalagmite. Beyond her a black-washed ceiling met the undulating floor.

A faint scuffle, like a commotion of doves, caused Ruth to turn her head. The wall to her left was rippling, swaying; blue ribbons, papers, photographs shivered in the draught and – a sudden sickness overcame her and she felt the blood drain to her stomach – she saw that among these were hanging limbs made of yellow wax: hands, feet, whole legs, women's breasts, shoulders – even a pair of hearts. There were surgical appliances, too, suspended among photographs and letters of thanks: wooden crutches, leg-irons, trusses, neck-supports – all heaving, shaking a little as if the whole wall were an invalid whose irregular breathing was dispersed into every trembling limb of her body.

Ruth moved along the wall with a fascinated revulsion, seeing the faded photographs of boys doing military service, of babies perched on cushions, reading the simple pieties: 'To the Virgin who saved my life', 'To the Mother of God from a mother whose prayers were answered', 'In deep gratitude for my husband's recovery', and in ballpoint, a spidery, barely legible 'Thanks'.

She became aware of a low murmur, like someone telling a rosary, coming from an inner room. It was a man's voice, speaking in a whisper:

'. . . It was here. The place was burned out completely. All the images, ornaments, confession boxes, the wax limbs of those days – it must have been an inferno . . .'

Instinctively her hand went out and touched the wall behind the tributes. The paint was the colour of soot. The voice – she recognised Eduardo – went on:

'My father didn't have time to come in and look around. Apparently he just ordered the soldiers who were with him to clear up. The old man said the flesh on the skeletons was like paper –'

'Oh!'

There was a rustle as the wax finger Ruth had inadvertently brushed off the wall slithered, lizard like, through the thicket of letters. It lay still on the stone floor. The voice stopped; Ruth wished she had not cried out – yet briefly it had seemed as if the finger were alive. The only thing to do was to bend down and pick it up by the ribbon; it had not cracked. Looking up she saw she was being watched by a plaster choirboy in a painted surplice holding an alms box.

'You?' José said.

The two of them were standing in the doorway to the inner room. Ruth's mouth dried; José's face was flushed with anger. Slowly his cousin came towards her in his anorak, his movements listless with exhaustion. As he stepped forwards she saw the bulk of a duffle-bag and a tweed jacket lying on a camp-bed beyond José. Somewhere something was banging – a bell-rope tautened by the wind.

'It isn't broken,' Eduardo said. With a slight groan he bent down and picked the finger up from the floor where she'd let it fall again. She took it from him and, her hand trembling, looped it up by its ribbon over a nail.

She was grateful when he spoke, for José's silence was terrible.

'What made you follow us?' he said quietly. 'You shouldn't have done that. I was talking something over with José . . .'

'I know, I'm sorry. I . . .' She wavered, blushing at the memory of the tape. She remembered why she was there.

'I thought I ought to warn you. Two men. In a jeep. They've been following since you left. Maybe it was me . . . Now they're down there –' She had addressed herself principally to Eduardo, who was still standing by the wall while José turned his back to them in the doorway.

Then José turned: he'd heard a squeal of hinges behind them. A sudden dampness rushed into the room, limbs and papers squabbling in the wind; the bell rope whipped against the wall.

The two men stood in the open door. One of them was wearing a denim jacket over a red sweater – Ruth recognised the driver of the jeep. But it was the one with the sticking-plaster who stepped forward. He was shorter than Ruth had expected, his black hair swept back above a face whose lower half protruded as if he had a peach in his mouth. His hands were thrust into the pockets of a grey mackintosh.

'Eduardo Cardona?' he asked.

Eduardo nodded.

'We've got a message for you,' the man continued. 'From a friend.'

What happened next occurred so quickly that, trying to piece it together later, Ruth found she recalled only fragments, and even these were not in the right order. She remembered slipping on the walkway and tearing her jeans; José's pale face as he grabbed her and pushed her down behind the car; Eduardo turning on the high path as the first shot rang among the cliffs. It was her terror, she supposed, which caused her to confuse the sequence of these moments so that only when going over them afterwards with José did she come to be able to put them in a sort of order.

It was Eduardo who moved first, rushing past them – did he shout out? – into the inner room as if something in the way the man had spoken convinced him of the need to run. Later Ruth asked herself if this had been the right decision, for it provoked an instant reaction in the two men who dashed in after him, but not before Eduardo had managed to grab something from the jacket on the bed. Then the second door was open – another slammed – and Eduardo was out in the rain with the two men running out after him.

She supposed that it was now that she felt José grabbing her arm so hard she cried out, as he pulled her back from the door and stepped out ahead; he must have called back to her for the next thing was their descent towards the car. Rain in her face, the planks muddy beneath her feet, she could scarcely control her helter-skelter plummet while from above cascades of rocks and pebbles bounced down from the cliff-top. Then she slipped and hurt herself, and José turned to raise her up, so that the sound of the shot caught them together and they were just in time to see the flap of Eduardo's anorak far up against the sky as he swung round, startled by the noise. Now they saw him pull out a gun himself and fire back in the direction of the two men scrambling after him between the rocks.

'Christ,' José said.

They were frozen for a moment by the sound; then another shot shattered the air.

How had they reached the car? Ruth remembered the feeling of tears coming, the uncontrollable shaking of her legs as they stood in the place José had dragged her to behind the creosoted hut, for Eduardo's pursuers were returning down the path. At that moment she didn't know if Eduardo had been shot or if he'd got away – it was only later that José told her that he'd parked his car at the top of a path down to the chapel in the rock. She shut her eyes with terror, her face buried in José's jacket, hearing the squelch of the pursuers' boots close beyond the hut. And not until she was in the front seat of Pedro's car with his arms around her did she realise that the engine noise she'd heard had been the two men driving off in the jeep. By then José was murmuring to her that it was all right, while the rain suddenly redoubled its tattoo on the roof of the car.

11

Sitting outside the civil guard post in the car, pressing the plaster she'd bought over the cut on her hand, Ruth realised she was not annoyed with herself for letting José go in alone to talk to the police. The important thing was that he'd given her the choice. It even seemed a means of indicating her gratitude for his not having blamed her for driving after them – and perhaps even showing Eduardo's pursuers the way – to admit that he didn't need her help in informing the civil guard.

Of course, José's anger had been overtaken by events. But it hadn't been clear to her until they drove up into this nondescript place – it was not a village she knew – that what they'd seen at the chapel was going to bring them together as it had.

She had still been shivering when he had driven them into a square, one side of which was a sturdy arcade; at the far end a stone balustrade stood over a river running between shallow banks. Opposite the arcade was a church between whose buttresses hung a shrivelled laurel wreath beneath the legend: *'José-Antonio Primo de Rivera ¡Presentes!',* and a list of the local falangists killed in the civil war.

'Well?' she had said, when he returned from the telephone booth. 'What did Elena say?'

'Not much.'

He fiddled angrily with the car's heater, and she could see that he was still annoyed; but she knew he needed to talk.

He went on, 'I phoned her last night after you came back – just to tell her Eduardo was OK and to reassure Teresa. I felt pretty stupid having to tell her it was no longer true.'

'Did you describe the two men to her?'

'She didn't know them. We couldn't ask Teresa because she'd gone for a walk.'

'And does she think we should tell the police?'

'Yes. She's promised to talk to Teresa about it. I'd have gone straight away. It's just that – I gave him my word.'

'He made Teresa promise that, too.'

José's only reply was to put the car into gear and roll it gently down the street towards the guards post they had passed on the way up. It was now that she had decided not to interfere: apart from feeling grateful to him she imagined he knew more than she did, and might not want to disclose it in her presence. She still felt curious, for the tape-recording had not clarified much, but she sensed that he might almost be ready to tell her what he knew, and she was prepared to wait. The events at the chapel had eradicated her impatience of the night.

She could see him now coming out beneath the gate, his breath pluming on the air. As he came up the street his face revealed a lack of confidence in the police.

'I told him what I could,' he said. 'Because it's Easter – only two men on duty. He said he'd phone Alcañiz if I wanted to wait.'

In the bar on the square a couple of men in blue overalls leaned against the counter while some more elderly ones played cards on a baize square near the stove. Seated at a marble table sipping a tumbler of coffee Ruth let her eyes follow the long trunk of the flue as it penetrated a window beyond which were the oak supports of the arcade. The wreath swung on the church wall.

José imbibed a little coffee, leaving a line of froth on his upper lip. He looked harassed and washed out, his chin covered in iron filings.

Ruth said, 'You promised to tell me what you know.'

He shrugged. 'Eduardo's in trouble – what more do you need

to know?'

'What more? Why – everything. What kind of trouble? Who are those people? Why were they following him?'

'That I can't tell you,' said José. 'Though I do have an idea . . .'

'And that horrible place – the chapel –?'

'I can tell you about that. Eduardo's father –'

'The nationalist?'

He stared at her. 'How did you know that?'

'I overheard you in that awful place – but also . . . I found his forage cap in the cellar up in Belmonte.'

'And the gun, I suppose?'

'Yes, it was so awful . . . Your sister told me it was his.'

'Well, towards the end of the war, when most of this area had at last fallen to the nationalist rebels, many of the defeated republicans took to the hills to avoid being shot. Some went underground – it was easy to find places to hide in the hills, and then local people – often their relations – would go up and leave food for them. Others managed to escape across the Pyrenees. When Eduardo's father returned to his wife's village her family house had been destroyed and only a farmhouse remained. Naturally, as head of the nationalist forces in that section, he was in charge of rooting out loyalists who had taken to the hills. You can imagine the rest.'

It was as though she could see it: the army lorries on the road, a sniper scrambling through the woods, too late to warn his comrades. She said, 'Had some taken refuge in that place?'

'Five of them, trapped, still hoping for reinforcements to arrive. Eduardo's father ran out of time – he was needed everywhere at once. It was he who gave the order to blow them out. The men who were with him were reluctant, so he threw the grenade in himself. He himself would never mention it, apparently, but last year Eduardo started to investigate his father's part in the war, and discovered this from one of the men who was with him – an old man who lives in one of the villages around here. A bit like your interviews, in fact. Does that answer your question?'

90

Ruth said nothing. She was thinking of that narrow aperture in the rock, the blast of death inside it, and the distant boom rumbling in the hills. She wondered if Eduardo's father had sweated as he turned away.

'One of my questions.'

José pursed his lips as he unwrapped a sugar cube and began to fold the paper very neatly.

'I still don't understand who the men are who followed him.'

'I told you I don't know.'

'But you've got an idea – you said so.'

'An idea – yes.'

He went on folding, his bottom lip caught between his teeth. Although she waited patiently she had a feeling his mind was working at something else – a further ramification of the issue she did not have enough information to comprehend. Finally he said, 'Why did you follow us?'

Why did I? she thought. But she managed to answer, saying how she'd felt left out the night before, how lonely it had made her and then, hearing them on the stairs . . .

Suddenly he interrupted: 'Eduardo told me last night that he'd been receiving these phone calls – and a typed message warning him he was being watched. He didn't know who they were from.'

'Perhaps that was what Teresa saw him burning.'

'Perhaps.'

'When did you meet?'

'Up at Belmonte yesterday morning. I wasn't expecting him. He just drove up looking out of it, and I gave him something to eat. He said he was concerned about something, but he'd rather not talk. Then he told me he wanted to go up to the chapel. At that time I thought he wanted to go up to look at it because of his father – it was only later that I realised he was thinking of it as a place to hide. I helped him search for someone who might have the keys. We had a lot of difficulty because to begin with we didn't know the priest's name. I was annoyed, but I felt I had to go.'

'You've been very good to him.'

'Do you think so?'

She nodded.

'There's still one thing I don't understand. If he was going to stay up there, how were you planning to get back?'

'He was going to drive me back to Alcañiz in the evening. He said there was something he wanted to tell me.'

'Don't you think it was wrong of him – to put your life at risk like that?'

'I don't think he knew the danger.'

'But he was armed. He must have done.'

José said nothing. The wind hooted in the stove's flue, making a sound like someone blowing across a milk bottle.

'Why did you decide to help him so much?'

A shrug. He had finished folding the sugar wrapper and as he lifted it on to his finger she saw that he had made a tiny paper stork. The lower part of his face almost smiled as he gently flapped the bird's wings. Then he gave it to her without a word.

She felt moved by the thing, remembering the real storks she had seen, returning in spring to build their ragged nests high on stone belfries in the towns of Castile. She had seen dead ones, too, from the train, caught on power cables, their wings swinging like rags.

A police van had driven up in the square outside.

12

It was a sight which would always stay with her, leaving an after-image on her retina like the jag of lightning on a dark sky, and indeed the water zig-zagged and stabbed down the overgrown crevice to strike the rocks far below with the force of an electric bolt before whirling, churning on beneath the bridge. It didn't matter that the sides of the abyss further down were scattered with detritus – detergent bottles, plastic sacks, even a tractor tyre, or that the stench of rotting vegetables rose up like smoke; Ruth clung to the iron pole of the railing, mesmerised by that abrupt break in darkness which seemed to her the beginning of life – the first splinter of light in chaos, pinning her to the rail. She felt a tremor pour down her spine: she'd seen the world's heart break, and she suddenly remembered the numbingly precise, the metronomical snap and scatter of a drum across the reservoir the day before. She knew now, too, that it was here, in the bar of the *albergue* over-arching the defile, that she had explained to José that night about wanting to go south.

Some time before, the old Simca had failed on a patched and pot-holed section of road just below the village. First the engine had developed a cough, then the car juddered in her hands, its wheels drifting on the road.

She and José had sat for a moment, hearing the rain tickle the roof while around them the light was beginning to die. Huge clouds loaded with night were already sweeping across the sky from the east. Suddenly Ruth felt lonely in spite of the presence of José.

'Pedro told me not to go too far.'

He itched his chin distractedly. 'It's probably the distributor.'

But they could do nothing. José peered under the bonnet at the old barnacled engine while she pedalled the accelerator, but all this produced was a hoarse, grinding shout. Not a single vehicle passed on the road.

The car's break-down seemed the last straw. Both she and José had been depressed by the trip up to the chapel with the guards, for looking round the place again had merely served to remind them of the malefic atmosphere it possessed. Then they had had to go to a guard headquarters in another village, so it was already late afternoon when they were finally free to return to Alcañiz. Ruth had not realised either, until now, how much Pedro's car had contributed to her feeling of security in relation to José. She saw now that, without knowing it, she had been proud of having provided their means of escape after the shooting.

They pushed the car on to the verge and, when the rain had let up, began to walk down the road between terraces of almond trees whose branches groaned in the wind. The church clock was already a pale electric disc when they entered the street beside the gorge.

Ruth had recognised the name of the village from the sign at the entrance to the place. It was set in a bowl of hills which was higher at one end of the valley; above the road to the left stood a jumble of breeze-block shacks with terracotta roofs backing on to mud tracks. The air was full of the squawk of hens and the bustle of caged doves, and there was a rich fragrance of pig manure and damp hay. Beyond the creeper-covered *albergue* on the far side of the chasm was another small hill with more shacks and the bell-stand of a tiny hermitage. The split in the ground reminded her of those renaissance pictures of the Last Judgement in which the revived dead are crawling out of the earth. On the far side of the narrow bridge a street of more solidly built houses mounted up; the tower of the church, an elaborate brick construction, looked as if it had been gnawed by rooks; grass and wall-flowers poked out of the cracks. The place stood at the end of the road, so the only way out was by returning the way you had come.

José was calling, already halfway up a street, and she had to tear herself off the bridge as if wrenching her finger from a cube of ice.

'I knew this place was familiar,' he said. 'Alfredo lives up here. I remember coming up to see him just before the sculpture exhibition.'

It seemed a distant memory: the rusted iron constructions on the library terrace, like the wrecks of ships; the little boy who clambered on to one for his parents to take a picture of him grinning in the sun. She had met Alfredo briefly at the private view in the town hall.

The sound of water shuddering in the gorge accompanied them up a street whose steps barely kept pace with a staggered row of señorial houses built on the proceeds of empire: carved coats of arms stood on arched doors; cast-iron centipedes squatted across windows.

The house José thought was the sculptor's took up the whole side of a cobbled street in which hens stalked, pecking for grain between the stones; it had the date 1640 on the lintel and a line of oak ribs supporting the gable. He had already given the bell-pull a tug and they had heard its racket deep inside; then a shutter opened in a ground-floor window and a little girl was standing in the space behind the bars. She looked about eight or nine, but it was difficult to tell, for her large brown eyes had the solemnity of children who have had to grow up too quickly.

'Wait,' she said. 'I'm coming.'

The cobbled hallway had a stone staircase rising out of it; to one side were a pair of iron rings for tethering mules.

José kissed the little girl.

'Hello. It's Alicia, isn't it? Is your father in?'

'Please wait a moment.'

She showed them into a room with long windows on to the street. It had the air of an exhibition space; on one of the walls was a series of black-and-white close-ups of the surface of fossils, each with a title on a card. Ruth remembered José once saying, 'This whole region used to be under the sea.' A pile of film-making equipment lay in one corner of the room: black camera cases, a pair of floodlights on stands.

José sighed. 'We should have phoned him –' he began, but at that moment the child returned, round eyes smiling, to say her father was in his studio and if they'd like to come this way . . .

They followed her through a shuttered room in which stood a gilded retable with saints painted on panels in a rococo manner: a girlish Saint George impaled a dragon; Saint Catherine rested her arm on her spiked wheel. Alicia said, 'Papá found that in a church they were demolishing.'

'Do you live here?' Ruth asked.

'No. I live with my mother in Barcelona,' she replied firmly.

They had gone down an exterior flight of stairs to a courtyard where a pair of cars were parked. Already they could hear the scream of a drill accompanied by a long rustling like the clatter of shingle in a breaking wave. Above them a weather-cock feathered the stream of clouds.

Alicia squatted down to stroke a black cat which had issued from the door.

'You go first,' she said.

They went past her into a room in which rusted shards of metal, bolted and welded together with deliberate roughness, flickered in the light of a shower of sparks. As their eyes adjusted to the darkness, the sculptures grew and diminished on the walls, the sparks' after-image glowing on the corroded hulks.

Stripping off gloves, goggles, Alfredo laid down the torch and came over to embrace José. He was as Ruth remembered him: a broad-shouldered, thick-set man with eyes like blue marbles and tufts of soft white hair not matching the metallic tint of his beard. His overalls were as patched as the iron plates.

'José! Finally you came! Why didn't you warn me –?'

'You remember Ruth?'

'Of course! Perfectly!'

Their breaths vanished on the air. José said, 'We're sorry to have interrupted –'

'Not at all. I was going to stop in ten minutes anyway. This week . . .' He sighed. 'I suppose Alicia's told you . . . ?'

'No.'

'Ah yes. Some friends of mine have got it into their heads to make a film about me. They're out now, thank God.' He called back into the room where an assistant, a young man in a blue boiler-suit was still at work.

In a large kitchen on the first floor Alfredo cleared a space on the wooden table, removing a full ash-tray, a stack of coffee glasses, while José telephoned from the room with the altarpiece: the sculptor had told him that as there was no proper garage in the village it would be best to get a mechanic from Alcañiz to come up in the morning. Ruth watched his huge hands, calloused and muscular from his work, almost swallowing the knife as he chopped a *chorizo* on a board. Then he opened a bottle of red wine and unwrapped some black olives from a piece of greaseproof paper.

The rough wine was comforting, though it tasted of her cold.

'How do you know José?'

'Oh, I don't know him well. He got in touch with me about that show at Alcañiz through his cousin.'

'What – Eduardo?'

'That's right. Do you know him too? He and I were at the Jesuits together in Madrid. After that I didn't see so much of him – I managed to get this grant to go to New York while Eduardo . . .' Alfredo smiled. '. . . He had his political activities. Not that I objected to that,' he went on. 'I was a paid-up member, too, in those days – I only quit in '77 at the time of all the in-fighting. Of course, when he got that radio job in Zaragoza we lost touch.' He took a sip of wine, then rubbed the tops of his thighs as if kneading bread. 'So what's he up to these days?'

They were interrupted by José coming back to say that Elena would pick them up. He threaded himself on to the bench beside Ruth.

'Alfredo and Eduardo were at school together.'

'Really?'

Already the wine had begun to go to her head; she took another slice of sausage and a morsel of bread to soak it up. Meanwhile José was briefly telling the sculptor what had happened with Eduardo. At some point Alicia reappeared, and her father swept her up to sit astride his knee as easily as she had picked up the cat.

When José had finished, he said, 'And you've no idea who these two blokes are?'

'He said he didn't know. He'd only tell me about the phone calls – and how he needed help.'

'What did they look like?'

José turned to Ruth for assistance. She could think only of the sticking plaster, which was useless, but he managed to say a bit more, although like her he'd barely seen them. Alfredo listened with attention while his daughter, who had slid to the floor, stroked the cat which rattled with pleasure under the table. Finally he said, 'No, I don't know them. But they're obviously bastards, whoever they are. More wine?'

Ruth had almost laughed with relief at the violence of his reaction; it was such a contrast to the gloom she and José shared. When he had filled up their glasses he said, 'I keep trying to think back to the last time I saw Eduardo . . . Now let me think . . . Oh yes – that would be in Madrid the year before last – at another of my shows. Didn't you get an invitation? That must have been – when? December, I suppose. I didn't have time to speak to him then – you know what these occasions are like, but the next day we went out for lunch. He told me he'd come into town to see his mother – a widow, apparently – and that his wife hadn't been able to come. That was a pity because I like her.'

'Did he come to the gallery on his own?' José said.

'I can't recall. I do know that when we met for lunch the next day he'd already had a bit to drink – you know Eduardo . . .'

He spat an olive stone into his huge hand and dropped it into an ash-tray. José, looking lean and uncomfortable, was drawing circles with his fingertip in a stain of wine on the wooden table. They seemed to have reached an unexpected hiatus in which Ruth was suddenly aware of a chaos of extraneous sounds – the screech of the weather-cock; the barking of tethered dogs, the purring cat at their feet. She even thought that, distantly, she could hear the rushing of the gorge. Then the noise retreated as her mind returned to the two men who were quite still, their eyelines bisecting in the ashes of the dead fire.

José had ceased to draw.

'Eduardo was a police spy, wasn't he?' he said.

For a moment Ruth doubted what she had heard. The word José had used was *topo* – mole; she remembered it from one of her interviews. She wanted to ask him how he had known, but Alfredo had already begun speaking slowly in a low voice, his thick hands on his thighs.

'It was something I'd suspected for a long time. And then that day in Madrid, he came out with it – drunkenly, when we were walking after lunch. In the restaurant I couldn't stop him drinking – he'd already told me something about himself, some personal information I didn't know what to say about. We went for a walk in the Casa de Campo after lunch. It had snowed, but I thought it would do him good to walk it off. Suddenly he began tugging at my sleeve, saying, "Alfredo – I want to tell you something." I said, "What?" And then he grabbed me, and he said, "You're just pretending you've no idea when in fact you – all my friends – have been laughing at me behind my back for years." Of course, I protested that it wasn't true, I didn't know what he was talking about. Then he said, "I want to tell you exactly – all the details, everything." At first I tried to shut him up. I knew he was drunk, and I thought it was going to be about some woman. Then he told me what you know. Anyway, I began to say the usual things you say to neurotic people – in our youth we all did things we regret. I even pointed out that the notion of collaboration with the regime was absurd in a sense because all of us – in some way – had been a part of it.'

The weather-cock squealed again outside.

He went on, 'I asked him if he thought his actions had caused anybody harm, and he said he expected so – I knew what the police were like, he said – still are like, sometimes. Then he fell silent. He was throwing stones on to the edge of the lake, skimming them on the ice. I told him to forget about it, but he said he couldn't. Not when everybody knew. He was convinced everyone knew.' He glanced at José. 'Obviously they didn't.'

José shook his head. 'I guessed,' he said softly. 'It had to be that.'

'I can't believe that Eduardo only spoke of it to me – he must have spoken to others – these men who you say he's with now, perhaps. He was convinced the people around him knew anyway. I found it all in a way so unnecessary, so ridiculous. After all, we've all done things we regret. If you get a woman pregnant you do whatever's necessary to accommodate the situation. You don't spend the rest of your life dwelling on it.'

José frowned. 'You think what he did was of no importance?'

'Not at all. Though I do believe that with time our perspective has to change; things which may have been criminal at one time now seem – well, less important. Besides, this may not be true of you because of your age but, as far as my generation is concerned, you only have to scratch a little at the surface to discover that not one of us is innocent.'

A few moments before, the doorbell had rung and Alicia gone again to answer it. Now Elena came in in a pale mackintosh, breathless from the stairs.

When she had greeted Alfredo, 'I've got news – Teresa's found something out,' she said.

13

Installed on the back seat of Elena's car as they passed the dead Simca on the road, Ruth remembered going up with her to the high cold city of Teruel the year before to obtain a resident's permit and wandering into a fair whose brightly-lit stalls, stitched together with a network of cables, floated in the mist about the town. They had wasted *duros* at a rifle-range, feeling the shock of the wooden butts against their shoulders as the revolving targets jerked from side to side. Finally, just when her attention had drifted, one of Ruth's shots got close enough to the bull's eye to slam down a target, earning Elena's congratulations and a panda in polythene which they managed to impose on a passing child.

Ruth had the familiar impression that, like the targets, the world had begun to jerk out of her sights and that she had lost the sense of belonging she had felt when José gave her the paper bird. This sensation had been reinforced by Elena's arrival, for when José was with his sister she sometimes felt as if, after the effort of learning his language, she had come across him using a dialect form of it to someone else: between them, so much seemed to go without saying. Besides, the urgency of Elena's news increased the speed of her delivery so much that, even without the roar of the heater isolating her from the two people in the front of the car, she might not have been able to follow every twist and turn of their dialogue.

Elena had not been able to start straightaway because almost as soon as she'd come in the sculptor had levered himself up from the table and excused himself, shaking hands warmly and asking them to let him know the outcome of the Eduardo business: 'I'd stay, but with this film . . . You've got my number. No, don't get up. You know the way out. Now, it's your bedtime, my love . . .' Seeing him hoist the little girl up into his arms, Ruth was seized with a desire to go with them – it was as though he had lifted up the room's warmth and were carrying it with him out of the kitchen.

As the brother and sister strode down the street, she almost had to run to keep up. She didn't want to interrupt, yet she could only catch fragments of their conversation above the gorge: '. . . Teresa was on her way back to Calanda . . . changed her mind . . . Aunt Emilia . . . Madrid . . .' Evidently Teresa had been talking to Eduardo's mother. Gradually, from these snatches and what she could hear from the back of the car, she began to assemble the bones of what Teresa had learned from the old lady.

It seemed that Eduardo had recently made several visits to an elderly gentleman in Madrid who had been a friend of his dead father. At first, these had gone well; the old man had even telephoned Eduardo's mother to say how delightful her son was – she suspected he wanted his money as the old man had no dependants and some land. Later Eduardo had lost his temper and threatened him, apparently, and on one occasion even broken a lamp or something. The old gentleman had gone round to see Eduardo's mother and told her that he was informing the police. He had also contacted his nephew, a member of Fuerza Nueva . . .

This mention of the fascist party surprised Ruth, for she had thought that it mainly existed nowadays in the minds of a few reactionaries and in the graffiti on walls; in the last elections it had gained only a single seat in parliament.

She wanted to lean forwards to ask why they thought Eduardo had been visiting the old man, but their tone had changed: José was doing most of the speaking now, his sister listening as she drove. Ruth could see her gold hair occasionally transformed into a halo by an oncoming car. The tension in José's voice suggested he was telling her what he had long suspected, even before the sculptor's confirmation, about Eduardo's link with the police, and she could tell that his mood was *sombra*; she could hardly interrupt them now.

She sat back, tucking her feet up beside her. The road was snaking upwards, and she thought the dark shapes above it had the flaky silhouette of mountain pines: Elena seemed to be taking a short cut back to Alcañiz. Whether it was the effect of the heater, the exhaustion of the day's events, or the combined frustration and reassurance of the back seat reminding her of holidays in her parents' car, she could feel herself drifting into sleep. And she did not wake until the sound of a buffeting wind on the body of the now stationary car had replaced the drone of the engine. She was on her own.

As she got out of the car a freezing blast of air shot through her like a train. The surface of her body was wide awake, although her insides were groggy; her legs staggered as she slammed the door. She felt sure she was high up – the wind had the dryness of the sierra; yet the deep square, taller than its ground area, made her feel as if she were at the bottom of an irrigation basin. Noble houses without ornament; a stone arcade covering a paved area containing a horse-trough; adjacent to this a row of wooden pillars sheltering a couple of shops. One of these seemed alive: a light glowed behind shelves of green and white pottery. At her back a massive building, whose sheer front in dark-grey brick was broken only by a huge arch, a row of great windows on the principal floor, and the long ribbed line of its oak gable, rose like a hinge of the night sky.

There were no other cars on the square: she got the feeling that this had long ceased to be the most important part of the town, fashion or convenience taking people elsewhere.

She rang the shop's bell, peering through to the light beyond the counter. Soon a grey-faced middle-aged man came towards her with a stained napkin tucked into his collar and a cigarette in his mouth, and began to unlatch the glass door.

She felt ridiculous as she said, 'Excuse me . . . I came with some friends . . . Have you seen them?'

He removed the cigarette with a frown, then gestured towards the night building on the far side of the square. He must have noticed her accent for he replied in a Spanish reserved for babies and foreigners: 'Over there. Big house? Understand?'

Returning across the square towards the car, she saw by the light of a street lamp a number one on a tin plate above the door and in faded black paint the words 'Casino Municipal'.

Ruth knew from her studies that a Spanish casino was not a gaming house – at least, not officially – but a club where the gentlemen of a town would gather in the evenings to smoke and re-read the day's newspapers. Before the war it had been a place for political debate, the scene of bitter feuds between liberals and moderates in the days of vote-rigging and *caciquismo* – the system by which a local man of mark mobilised by fair means or otherwise the votes of a constituency on his candidate's behalf. It was a place of continuity and male solidarity, where the old waiters knew a member's preferences: she had an image of a tray with black coffee and a glass of iced water being brought to a charcoal-suited gentleman in a wicker chair; in a poem by the republican poet Machado, an old man in the casino had stood for the intellectual and political degeneracy of the country.

A small door set into the great one was not locked; she found herself in an entrance hall, one end of which opened on to a courtyard. There was a smell of damp masonry and rotting wood. To her right a flight of stairs led up around a gigantic iron lantern whose bulb cast the shadows of its struts over crumbling plaster walls. Somewhere in the building's depths a shutter banged.

On the first floor the stairs faced a large double entrance with, at one side, a glass door standing slightly ajar; smashed tiles and rubble lay beyond. Next to the stairs was a polished oak door with a brass relief of St Christopher on it above a grille for peeping at strangers. This door was slightly open, and from it came a creak of floorboards and the murmur of voices. Although the hall was not lit, Ruth could see an oil painting opposite the door of what looked like a Christ child standing on a pedestal surrounded by the faces of four angels.

She recognised the voice of Elena. The other voice had the strident timbre of a local woman.

'. . . You'd have expected him to be here?'

'Well, yes, of course – when I saw him on Saturday he told me he was going to stay for Easter, which he usually does . . .'

'You don't do any of his cooking for him, then?'

'No. He always goes down to the gentlemen's club for his main meal, and the rest he does himself.'

She heard José intervene. 'Did you say he goes to the gentlemen's club? Isn't this –?'

'No, this is the *former* gentlemen's club. The new one is that modern building on the Valencia road – you probably saw it as you came in.'

Elena again. 'Doesn't he have any family in town?'

'Not since his sister died – oh, that must have been three years ago, at least . . . I thought you were relations?'

'Just friends.'

There was a low murmur; Ruth suspected that José was conferring with Elena out of earshot of the housekeeper. Then he said, 'Yes, you see the thing is, my sister has tried to phone him a couple of times in Madrid, too, and has had no reply . . .'

'Oh, I see. That's strange. You see, I'd usually have come in today but, as it was my son's first Communion, I asked if I could come in tomorrow instead . . . What's strange is that he can't have gone far because his car's in the patio – and, besides, his stuff's all here, isn't it? Look – there's his suitcase . . .'

They began talking about the police. The building intrigued Ruth; she knew the historical importance of casinos, but she had never been inside one before. She reckoned that the others would be a few more minutes at least with the talkative housekeeper; besides, they would not leave without her. Pushing open the glass door, she stepped through on to the tiles beyond.

A gust of cold air came forwards to greet her and she realised she was on a gallery protected from the interior patio by a row of wooden shutters. One was loose, and through it came a swaying patch of moonlight broken by clusters of leaves. Beyond an archway at the far end lay an antechamber; more rubble cluttered the floor, and a gigantic framed canvas leaned with its face to the wall. Finding the book of matches in her pocket, she lit one and cupped it in her hand, seeing the flicker of a decorated plaster ceiling. In places the floor was so uneven that she had to edge forwards with care to avoid falling through a hole.

The light of the match, as it died, had revealed an expanse of darkness through a pillared archway to her left. Striking another, she got the impression of a very long room with a pair of doors at the extreme end; five huge shuttered windows gave on to the street. Dark shapes, the carcasses of sofas and stacked chairs, danced and expanded. She became aware of a smell of dust and rancid cheese, and she felt sure that above the scrape of the magnolia leaves on the gallery shutter she could hear the scuffle of rats.

The flame turned blue and went out, and in her attempt to strike another she lost the book. When she bent down to search for it among the rubble her hand encountered something solid: a cold metal object with a piece of wood attached – a bunch of keys. As she picked it up something settled briefly on her hand. At that moment she jumped with alarm – she had heard a loud crash just behind her. She calmed herself; it was the shutter slamming in the night wind. Its creak, formerly disquieting, reassured her now.

There was a shuffle and a murmur of voices ahead of her through the double doors.

Fear fell on her like a net; in the same instant she understood – the doors ahead gave on to the stairs.

'José! Elena!' she shouted, her voice feeble in the vast rooms. Suddenly she was seized by an overwhelming need to escape: she had had enough of the inexplicable noises, the fetid air. The quickest way out was via the end doors; even if they were locked she must attract the others' attention or she might have to spend the night in the town.

She moved forwards; suddenly she trod on something soft, and she had the feeling it had moved; then she was down, struggling to be free of the heavy cold mass on to which she had fallen and which with the shock of her weight seemed to have risen briefly to embrace her. A dry lizard-texture brushed her cheek. She began to scream. And she went on screaming until she saw the flame of a cricket lighter in the room on to the gallery; then she heard Elena and José calling her name as they came forwards to where she was crouched by the dark doors, crying now, her toad's heart pulsing.

Elena's face flickered as she bent down over the thing Ruth had stumbled on. 'Oh my God . . .'

The flame shook in her hand: seeing Elena's fright somehow helped her to control her own. José said nothing, but she could feel his arm tremble as he hugged her.

Elena's voice said, 'We must go to the police.'

'Yes.'

Later, down in the square, Ruth saw the man from the shop crossing the road in his slippers with another neighbour, was aware of José putting his coat around her shoulders as someone got into the car with Elena, felt the weight of the keys in her pocket and took them out to give to José; his pale hand closed around them.

Then he was murmuring something – giving her instructions; meanwhile thoughts flowed through her mind in no order – of Eduardo, of the keys to the chapel, of the conversation in the car; her first idea had been that the dead man was his father, but he had died long before. Nothing made sense. She knew only that the story of Eduardo's troubles, which she had assumed was drawing to its close, had only just begun.

Suddenly she was alone, walking as fast as she could out of the square towards the source of the wind: a high terrace over the town with a long balustrade. When she saw this she began to run and went on running, leaving behind her a long terrace of houses with wooden balconies and a saint's statue in its niche. She reached the balustrade and gripped the stone, taking great gulps of night air.

A trace of snow dusted her lips. She shut her eyes, and it felt as if little by little her face were flaking off into small pieces; she imagined her whole body disintegrating, the tiny dry fragments scattering and dancing on the wind.

PART THREE

THE DRUMS

14

They had begun while she was writing in her notebook. Far away and still concentrated mainly in the Plaza de España, their rumble was so quiet that it was drowned by the slightest movement in the room – the rattle of a pane, the springs of the divan. You might forget it until a silence you created allowed it to return.

Ruth opened the window and the sound poured instantly into every corner of the room. It had two strands – a deep tremor flecked on its surface by the metallic spark of snare-drums. Carried on the wind, it seemed to have a force inside it, driven on like mist unravelling across a landscape.

Two young women were standing on the pavement just below the window. They were stocky, ugly girls, drums suspended loosely from their shoulders; they had paused for a moment in their progress towards the main square to do up the buttons on the tunic of a little girl who waited patiently, a smaller drum hanging down her back. While one of them was doing this the other adjusted her headgear in the wing-mirror of a parked motor-bike – a satin cap like a surgeon's with a long tongue of the same material, pleated crosswise, falling down behind. The wind caused the caps' tongues and tunics to shimmer against their limbs.

Closing the window, she went into José's room to make the bed. As she pulled it together she thought how much had changed since her return from the south. In the penitential mood she'd been in then she'd anticipated – indeed almost desired – recriminations from José, or at least the abandonment to silence of which she knew he was capable. Eduardo had made a confrontation impossible, and when the shooting had flung them together the restraint José had shown wasn't evidence that he'd forgiven her, only that more important things were on his mind. Since she'd forced herself upon him, he'd decided to resign himself to sharing them with her. Logically, she supposed now, it should have made her uneasy that the answers to the questions which had preoccupied her on the journey back had merely been postponed. But in practice she no longer felt the need to bother him about them; the proof of this was that his absence now – he had once again had to go and speak to the *guardia* – did not disturb her.

The linen counterpane billowed and fell over the bed. She smoothed its wrinkles, then ran a hand through her hair in the wardrobe mirror. What had brought the two of them together again, she wondered, if not deeply, at least enough to provoke the soft creases of a smile about her eyes? She decided it was the unpleasant experiences they had undergone together. They had practically shared the discovery of the body, and throughout the tedious hour or so of police procedure which followed she'd been conscious of his emotional state as well as her own. Hers was of physical shock – even now she could feel the rasp of the dead man's cheek on her face; José's was a deep gloom, for if, as seemed certain, it was Eduardo who had shot the old man, José's attempts to help him had been in vain. For her own part, her last image of Eduardo – the smudge of his anorak on the skyline as he turned to fire at the two men – had been replaced in her mind by another: she saw him tumbling down a long streak of water into a bottomless ravine. If that was her image, what worse picture haunted José?

As she ran a bath she saw the paper stork among the things emptied from her jeans pockets the night before. A small measure of her guilt over the secret recording returned at the sight of it; it seemed better to console herself with the thought that she'd refrained, on several occasions now, from harrowing him, such as that morning when she hadn't insisted on accompanying him to the civil guard

112

headquarters in Alcañiz.

When she turned off the taps the drumming was a muffled echo in the inner courtyard. It sounded like the bounce of ping-pong balls in a vacuum pump.

The hot water, enveloping her, soothed and began to extract from her limbs what remained of the pain in her belly, now a tingling numbness. Lying there and seeing the slight distortion of her body by the water she had a sudden vision of the reservoir that summer when she had felt complete and alive, her soul defined by the dry heat and cool, deep water, and floating on her back had seen a sparrow-hawk dreaming on the air. She began to think again about the questions concerning José and her which had been postponed. There was a feature of José's character, she reflected – perhaps it was because he was older than she was, which allowed him to accept things more as he found them, while having the patience to work methodically, relentlessly for change. He was not hot for certainties as she was, but prepared to live with the provisional. Was it being brought up in the country which had endowed him with this equilibrium? The city, she decided, was her unnatural habitat.

She had travelled south to find out about José. She knew this now, and it was a paradox that she'd only come to recognise this aspect of what she'd done after the various things which had brought them together had played their part. Ideally, perhaps, they would have remained separate, given themselves time to consider the implications her journey south had for both of them. But too many factors – not only the troubles of Eduardo, but José's equanimity and her own need, after the south, for physical acceptance, as well as her determination to make a decision about their future – were working against this. And that was the true reason, she realised now, why she hadn't needed to go to the police with him. It hadn't been discretion at all, but the security of their once again being available to each other.

Yet there was a difference, she thought, between the way things had been before and how they were now. Now Tom did not represent a threat the stakes were higher; she could no longer blame someone else for her inability to make up her mind. Of course, she could always make everything dependent on her work, which had its own timescale. Would she return to England to write up her material and return here in a year or so's time? Would José come with her? How unrealistic the notion of a definite answer to these questions seemed. Yet she felt the lack of such an answer as acutely as she had felt the absence of an element in the landscape. And because of the kind of man José was, and because of his way of loving her, she knew that she was going to have to resolve the matter on her own.

After dressing she returned to the kitchen and made a late lunch out of some undressed salad and cold chicken left over from the evening before. Halfway through the meal she remembered it was Good Friday, and that she ought to have been eating fish. This echo of religious observance reminded her of the anarchists' onslaught on the influence of the Church, a policy which was in a way contradictory, because anarchism itself presupposed a quasi-religious community of the faithful. She reminded herself to make a note of the idea that the burning of churches could be interpreted less as an attack on Christianity than on the symbols of reaction.

A sudden explosion led her to the window. A group of drummers were slouching along the street, their long tunics inhaling the wind. The sound, which whipped up like a breaker against a cliff, was oddly out of phase with their strong, rollicking pace. They swung back, still drumming, to let a car pass, then fell back into step with the casualness of dancers in a routine.

She had almost forgotten the strange ceremony in the maelstrom of the past days. By now the *rompida* – the moment when all the drums began together at a signal from a balcony – would have taken place in some of the other towns or villages. In her bedroom she flicked through her notebook to find the page on which she had once tried to list all the possible explanations of the ceremony she had heard: its Arabic origin, its connection with the spring equinox . . .

Suddenly there was a repeated buzz inside the tattoo: the doorbell. She yelled into the entryphone: 'Who is it?'

'Police,' a man's voice said. 'We're investigating the case of a stolen car . . .'

Then she relaxed into a smile. Pedro was in the doorway, his chin smooth over the shadow, fragrant with aftershave, the hair brushed back from his handsome face. A side-drum hung over his shoulder.

'Yes, regarding this car, madam . . .'

She blushed, and he touched her arm.

'It's all right. I spoke to Elena yesterday and she told me that you've been having a bad time, all of you.'

'Did she explain?'

'Not really.'

His ignorance of it all was another reason for liking him.

'I wouldn't know where to begin.'

'That's all right. I meant to call round before but – no time. So José's back now?'

'Yes – he's out. There may be some beer . . .'

He shook his head. 'No, I came to see if you and he would like to come to Calanda to the drums. My brother and I are meeting some friends down at the workshop at about nine. It'll be a squeeze, but if you like –'

'I'd love to, but . . .'

Extraordinary as the ceremony was, she couldn't face it that night; anyway, José would soon be back, and she wanted to hear if there was news. As Pedro stepped back on to the landing a car horn blared below.

'Go on,' he said. 'We're going to join in. You can borrow a drum.'

'Sorry, Pedro.'

'It's a bad sign.' But he grinned as he began to stride down the stairs. Towards freedom, she thought, towards his physical life, his honest wanting and taking, towards the barrage of the drums.

She called out as he reached the landing, 'That car . . . I know you told me not to take it further than Belmonte . . . We'll get it back to you for sure.'

'Of course. After Easter. I would never have lent anything decent to a driver like you . . .'

She heard the slam of the door below, and the street muffled behind it.

On returning to her bedroom she had second thoughts. She felt well enough – or nearly. When José came back he might not have any news. Was it cowardly of her not to go?

Down below, through the window, she could see the traffic trapped in the tiny square making a cacophony of hooting above the splash of passing drums. Pedro had gone, but his truck would be stuck down there with the others, jerking forwards a few metres a minute . . .

She remembered why she'd come into her bedroom. But instead of turning straight to the notes she'd made on the ceremony she began to ruffle through the book's pages, skimming some passages and rejecting others – a habit of hers. For she'd discovered that it did not matter that periods of her life were absent, or only partially to be gleaned, from the notebooks she kept; they were there in silhouette and, looking through them, an outline of herself emerged. It was like a comic book she had owned as a child in which, when you rifled rapidly through the pages at one corner a phantom horseman appeared and began to ride in jerks, lashing his horse on the way.

15

12 September

> 'The sleep of reason produces monsters.'

An embarrassing incident today. I was in the middle of an
interview in Calaceite – a very old woman whose family
had been 'individualists', in other words they'd chosen to
remain outside the collective and work alongside it – when
a middle-aged man burst through the door, obviously very
drunk, shouting. 'Mother! What the devil are you doing?
How dare you speak to this foreign whore?' etc. He tried to
grab my tape-recorder, luckily I got away just in time;
then, to my horror, he turned on the old woman and began
to bundle her out of the kitchen. I'd have got involved if
another person – his wife, I suppose – hadn't appeared and
interposed herself between them; still, she couldn't prevent him from shouting at me, so there was nothing for it
but to leave.

How to persuade people who've lived most of their lives
under the dictatorship that there's no longer any risk in
talking about the war? On the way back I parked the van
and got out, realising I was more shaken than I'd thought.
A sudden sense of hopelessness about my work. I feel that
all I'm doing is interfering in people's lives, not giving
them anything, as José is for example. He was very good to
me when I got back, saying I mustn't expect it to be easy –
my work is worthwhile – and that anyway I've done too
much to go back now. Stupidly I've just rejected him,
slamming the door and coming in here to write this,

simply because – I think he knows this – I'm envious of what he does. I long so much for a way to wrench my work out of the past.

18 September

Out here I see things more clearly. Not confused by the complexity of my feelings about England, I can see the actions of others, and my own, framed in a vacuum of ignorance. And as I work to fill the vacuum I feel I have some control over the growth of my understanding. It's like a second chance to grow up. I remember the sensation, on my first visit to Teruel, that here was a place where things were complete and in some way objective. I felt as if I were seeing the world three-dimensionally for the first time.

'There are no this year's birds in last year's nests.' This proverb is spoken by Don Quijote to Sancho on his death-bed. The joke – there's always a joke with Cervantes – is that, having complained bitterly about Sancho's endless quoting of proverbs, the old man is using one himself.

6 October

Is it possible to have a 'pure' reason for doing anything? It seems that I only have to look twice at anything I've done to find a second or third motive underneath the one on the surface. Coming out here, for example. I wrote on my grant application form that I needed to investigate the collectives because the other research I'd seen on them seemed insufficient and was of a different kind. This was true, but I was remembering José all the time. I wanted to show Tom – and myself – that I was strong enough to do without him. I wanted to return to a place where I'd been happy. I loved the landscape . . . There would probably be more reasons if I looked more closely. And the odd thing is that each one of them is true.

After tea

My fear of not belonging. I know it's exaggerated, but that doesn't make it go away. It leads me astray so that I feel like a beggar or a prostitute.

José's cousin Eduardo was up at the village house this weekend with his wife Teresa. As usual his only way of approaching me was through jokes about being English – the Queen's corgies, my wanting tea . . .

I remember José once telling me that Eduardo was unhappy, but he wouldn't tell me why. It occurs to me that it's also possible to be a foreigner in your own country. If that's how Eduardo feels the jokes about Englishness could be a way of comparing us. As if my problems were distant cousins of his.

15 October

Walked up the steep road to the castle. The sky a high blue, almost cloudless, the hills an arena of red and brown; I could hear the city beneath: the boys screaming in the yard of the Escolapios, their football banging on wire mesh. No wind in the pine trees. Down to the east orchards above the river through a network of telegraph wires. It was lying in the dust and dirt of the slope, the body of its friends twittering on the air – a goldfinch, tawny sheened, still bleeding from its neat wound; shot for fun, I suppose, from the terrace of one of the houses beneath. There were no shots anymore, only the dead creature in my hand, the wind in the dry grasses, stones giving way under my feet. I scrabbled a hole in the rocks and buried it there, in a shallow grave, hoping to save it from the hawks.

3.00 p.m.

I've just woken from a deep sleep and want to write down this dream straight away before it goes. I was lying on the floor of a troop-train surrounded by young men, many of whom were wounded and had their arms or faces in bandages. There were no seats in the carriage so some of them were huddled on the floor sleeping, some smoking, some flapping at their faces to keep off flies. One near me touched my arm and pointed out a soldier who was lying with his back to us, saying, 'He's dying'. When I got up and tried to pull down a blind he rose to help me; in both our hands for a moment the blind struggled like a bird. Then it came down and we were in darkness.

José was on the train and I knew I had to find him. I had my tape-recorder strapped over my shoulder and began going through the carriages, stepping over bodies, asking the men, 'Do you know a soldier, name of Alejos? He's Aragonese.' They shook their heads. 'Hey comrade –' one said, 'I know an Alexey, but he's Russian – what do you want him for?' The train drew up at Caspe station. It was dawn and I could see the high church with its empty windows. A bell clanked and the train pulled away and I entered the station building, where a lot of people with luggage were sleeping, waiting.

One of them, standing in front of me, was in uniform. It was José. He took me out into the forecourt – a wide, dusty place with many people lying on stretchers under sheets. There was a clock on the station tower.

José pointed to the centre of the forecourt where a man was dragging something along the ground. He was practising bull-fighting passes with a stick as the *muleta* and an old jacket as the cape. The movements were fluid, delicate – the only thing we could hear was the scrape of the jacket against the ground trailing in the dust.

23 October

Out with José this evening in the ploughed fields outside Alcañiz where once English troops met the French in the war of independence. Someone had said there were musket-balls, but we didn't find one. The fields were in shadow – above us the hills so bright in the setting sun it was as if the light were inside them. Suddenly a flash and we were dazzled by a bright point of light which came and went. Someone – we don't know who – was playing with a piece of mirror out there, picking us out in the shadow of the hills.

Writing this has reminded me of another time when we drove up to the top of a village perched on a hill, full of fluttering washing, breeze-block houses braced against the wind. I could see José sitting down below on a bench beside a screeching swing while I took a path up above the church tower to the top of the hill. It was a walled cemetery, a square crown full of brambles and subsiding graves. I couldn't help remembering a dreadful story an old man told me the week before of how, when a place in this region was on the point of falling to the nationalists, the republicans, before retreating, dug up some of the bodies in the cemetery and arranged them up there in a dance of death to greet the victorious rebels.

As I walked down the hill to find José the earth crumbled under me and, reaching out to save myself, I found I was clutching at a hill of human bones: the earth was solid with hard yellow scraps.

19 November

Visited Belchite this morning. I'd heard so much about the place and wanted to go before, but had never got round to it. José didn't want to go – in fact, I had to do a lot of persuading to get him to make the small detour when I saw it on the map as we were coming back from Zaragoza today. 'The small detour' – that sounds like a tourist, and it may have been that feeling, the same feeling of voyeurism I sometimes get in my interviews, that sickened me when we got there.

After the turn-off, the road runs straight for several kilometres, a single line of telegraph-poles between fields of stubble under the sky. At first sight the church and other buildings could belong to any other village south of the Ebro – it's only as you get closer that you see that they are empty shells, shattered from endless bombardment. And the ruined walls and church tower, against the moving clouds, seem to be travelling towards you. I'd expected José to stay in the van while I looked around, but I found I didn't want to get out. I felt it would have been like seeing an accident on the road and looking to see if there's blood. That feeling, and an emptiness, too. A sense of waste.

I've just looked up what actually happened. On the edge of the nationalist zone in the first year of the war, Belchite was the village which held out the longest against the republican advance in the autumn of '37, not surrendering until 6 September. It was besieged again the following spring, this time by the nationalists during the Aragón campaign which ended in their reaching the sea. In spite of strong fortifications designed by the Russian Colonel Bielov, the village was retaken in March 1938. It was Franco who decreed that it should not be rebuilt, so that it should stand as a memorial – and warning – to future generations.

Of course, Franco's aim was political. But I can't help being reminded of Dalí's macabre proposal to the nationalists at the end of the war to set up a line of skeletons along the road from Madrid to the Escorial, an idea typical of his determination to shock, and either infantile or brilliant, depending on your opinion of the man.

18 February

I'd forgotten the drums until a few days ago I came across a group of men rehearsing out on the terrace above the town. There were about ten or twelve of them, young and middle-aged, facing inwards, glancing across the circle to each other while they played, alert to changes in speed or rhythm. The drums hang at waist level, like match-sellers' trays. But what was really strange was the way the men's faces looked almost expressionless, as if they were spectators at their own performance.

I stayed there for a long time, just listening to the shifts and variations in rhythm and volume. These were partly produced by the players, and partly the result of deflection by the buildings around: at one moment the sound seemed to be coming from the drums themselves and at another from the wall of the church. It was like a kaleidoscope, chucking audible flakes one on top of each other with each twist. Suddenly I had this picture of all the fragments of my life gathering together and starting to listen and shout to one another like the sticks on the skins. When the sound was solid the picture would vanish again.

I've heard the following possible explanations of the drums:

a) Pagan/Iberian. A ritual marking the spring equinox, intended to drive out evil spirits and ensure a good harvest. A seasonal fertility rite.

b) Islamic/North African, from the time of the Moorish occupation. Drums common among the tribesmen of North Africa.

c) Medieval. The commemoration of a signal warning the inhabitants of the recently reconquered towns that the Moors were returning to reconquer lost territory.

d) One of the above rechannelled into a Christian ceremony, like those Christian churches built on ancient sites (sacred springs, burial mounds) whose symbol is very often St George slaying the dragon of the old religion.

This ceremony having a penitential significance – like the flagellants in Easter processions elsewhere, marking the period between the death of Christ on the cross and the Resurrection. A representation of the 'darkness over the face of the earth', earthquakes, the veil of the temple being ripped. Religious guilds form the core of the drummers.

This ceremony, which had fallen out of use, revived in the twentieth century by a local curate, Mosén Vicente Allanegui.

e) A protest, disguised as a religious ceremony, of Spanish villagers against the occupying French soldiers during the war of independence.

f) A protest, when the town was in the hands of the anarchists during the civil war, by the inhabitants of Calanda against the banning of the drums along with other forms of religious observance. (An absurd ban, because it would be difficult to imagine a more co-operative occasion, in which everyone – men and women of a town or village – contributes to a communal celebration; but the anarchists' assault on the church was one of the causes of the war.) In protest against this ban all the members of the town joined in, making it impossible for any individual to be prosecuted. Like in Lope de Vega's play *Fuenteovejuna* in which the villagers escape punishment for the murder of the local squire by insisting, under torture by the inquisition, on corporate responsibility for the killing.

g) A religious ceremony containing an element of popular protest, during the Franco era, against the oppression of the dictatorship. In the immediate post-war period the crowds of drummers gathered for the *rompida* enabled members of the resistance hiding in the sierra to return to their towns for a few hours unrecognised by the authorities.

These are all the explanations which, with José's help, I've gathered together, and I'm sure there are more. I must say that I don't find any one of them entirely satisfactory. I can't say why, but as I was writing this a line by Octavio Paz from a book of his poems which has just arrived in the library came back to me:
'Truth,
Is the depths of time without history.'
No idea what this means. And of course it sounds better in Spanish (Don Quijote, coming across a copy of Part One of his own story in a Barcelona bookshop, remarks to

Sancho that reading a book in translation is like seeing a
Flemish tapestry from behind).

24 February

On the way back from Mas de las Matas after today's interview I saw a hermitage on a small hill and decided to park
the van and walk up to it. A dusty path wound up and
round a rocky hill studded with yews and cypress. The
little stone box was at the top, with an arched terrace.
Through a window in the door I could see an empty room
with an altar with a linen cloth on it, and a plaster statue of
a saint with a hand on her heart. There was nothing up
there except a few brambles and the scent of cypress.

At some point I remembered that it was the very place
which José and I visited when I came out to visit him
during a vacation and where he told me about his brother
for the first time. We were talking about Orwell's *Homage
to Catalonia* which I'd brought with me, and how the
international communist party had crushed the more
indigenous one to which Orwell was affiliated, just as later
they crushed the anarchists.

'My brother was a party member,' he said.

I suppose I said, 'I didn't know you had a brother',
because I'm pretty sure he replied, 'I don't. He died, after
being involved in a demonstration. That is, we're not sure
. . .'

I remember looking at his face. He wasn't even looking
at me, and I felt how, for me, Spain's history was merely
an object of study. When he looked up his eyes were wet.

Perhaps it was then that I fell in love with him? I know I
asked him all sorts of banal questions, to which he replied
politely. His parents were in Belmonte and could do
nothing, though his father came to Madrid and pestered
the authorities for a while. This was against his mother's
wishes – she forbade them to mention Juan when she
found out about the demonstration. It was impossible to
do anything in those days. José was only sixteen when it

happened. We rehearsed this conversation, but all the time I was thinking: I love this man. That was the time when I came alone to Teruel.

1 March

'History to the defeated
May say Alas but cannot help or pardon.'

I thought of these lines by Auden from his poem 'Spain' as a possible epigraph to my thesis. Reading a footnote about them I see that later Auden repudiated them – presumably he'd come to believe that history did have some redemptive power.

He also altered those verses of the poem which advocated violence. For English intellectuals of the thirties the civil war was a symbol of the struggle for the soul of Europe between democracy and fascism. Yet, in the course of the war, as Orwell describes, the democratic forces became (out of necessity, for they could not have done without Soviet arms) instruments of Stalin's foreign policy.

Lots of English writers about Spain are motivated by shades of the idealism of the thirties – I suppose I'm no exception. In my most foolish moments I've imagined my name on one of those long banners hung up to commemorate the heroic deaths of members of the International Brigades: Lukácz – Hungary, Cornford – England, and so on. A ridiculous idea. Especially as I understand better, now, the unfashionable doubts which caused Auden to flee this country so soon after his arrival in '37, and Hemingway's final disillusionment with both sides in the conflict. When a war begins, no one is innocent any more. At least there's no doubt in my mind that after forty years of dictatorship Spain needs a period of reconciliation. The words of the exiled president of the republic, quoted by Hugh Thomas: 'Peace, pity, pardon.'

Train. Linares – Granada. 9 March

The little girl at the pool's edge. Why do I remember this now, though I don't know the source of it – a dream? a childhood memory? She must be seven or eight, with scruffy hair and gypsy skin, in a worn-out printed dress. She walks down the shadow side of an earth street to a pool overhung with aloes and fig trees. The pool is stagnant, quite still – tiny midges float on its surface. She picks up a stone and throws it – the ripples slowly devolve.

Granada. 23 March

Walking in the gardens of the Alhambra yesterday evening I came upon that old verse, on a plaque on the creeper-covered wall: 'Give him alms, woman, for there can be no greater poverty than to be blind in Granada.'

I went into the church as a refuge, searching for some peace after all that's happened here, but when I got in I saw it was packed – there were even people standing at the back, while a priest addressed us from the altar on 'the sense of sin'. All around him were masses of white lilies and carnations. I'd stopped listening to the sermon and was just drinking in their scent when I heard a throaty cry ahead of me. An old man was standing by the gates of a side chapel in a pair of blue workman's trousers and an old tweed jacket. He'd begun speaking, not in time with the priest but in a drunken rhythm of his own, shouting unintelligibly. At first people ignored him among the din of babies and shuffling feet; then they looked awkwardly round, with embarrassment more than anger. I could hear the priest's voice arching from speaker to speaker: 'Everywhere – in schools – at work, in the world of the media, we have lost our sense of sin because we have forgotten that we are lost . . .' The drunk's voice came, shouting, 'You're all lost – all of you!'

I couldn't help smiling, but at the same time it annoyed me that my enjoyment had been reduced to curiosity. The question now was who would win, the priest or the drunk. Then a young chaplain came up and, kindly and gently, with his hand on the old man's arm, led him out, saying, 'Please come outside. Please come. You're disturbing the Mass. Please come with me.'

Something made me follow them out on to the steps where the argument continued, the chaplain's surplice fluttering in the breeze. 'You're drunk too!' 'You were disturbing the others.' 'It's my right.' 'Not during Mass . . .'

As I watched I thought of the lovers being sent out of paradise; it occurs to me now that the priest was wearing the harassed face of democracy.

Alcañiz. Good Friday.

Still frightened now, after last night, though I've had time to recover. The thought of that casino and what I found there makes my hand tremble as I write. The strange thing is that sitting on a camp-bed in the housekeeper's spare room and waiting for José to come back was almost worse than what happened in the place itself. I suppose it was because I was beginning to understand the meaning of what I'd seen.

Now it still troubles me to think of it, but I'm only partly afraid, as if I could see what happened as if it were an old silent film flickering on a screen. More than anything I remember Eduardo's face in the church. Of course I'd tried to imagine before what it would be like to be a murderer. But I think it was at that moment that, even without knowing what he'd done, I saw how a person can be trapped by an action he or she has taken. Yet, basically, I've always believed that we can find a way out of the labyrinth of the past – but only by confronting it, not by running away.

A hand on her shoulder. Ruth felt herself blushing, and at the same time moved her hand out to close the book – then stopped. There was nothing to be ashamed of in what she'd written. A moment before she'd felt the pressure of lips on top of her head, as if a flame burned there and went out. She hadn't looked round. Then José's hand moved down her arm from her shoulder to catch her own hand. She leaned back and rested her head against him.

'Are you all right?' he asked.

'How did you get on at the police station?'

'There's still no news of Eduardo. I told them to find out if those keys you picked up belonged to the curate, but they still haven't contacted him. They kept saying, "It's Easter". As if that meant there could be no police service!'

'Have you told them everything?'

'Elena has.'

'Including what Alfredo said?'

He nodded, then moved to the window, a hand in his pocket.

There was a rustle of drums in the street below. Staring down, he said, 'It was something I'd suspected for a long time. I couldn't mention it to him while I didn't know. I think what made me sure was him saying he'd got something he wanted to tell me. As you heard.'

Ruth blushed again. The evening before, after supper, she'd admitted making the recording. It had seemed the right moment – when he was holding her in his arms and comforting her after a sudden recurrence of fear. And, indeed, it was his forgiving her that had given the final impetus to their reconciliation.

'What about the old man's family? Have they been told?'

'The housekeeper's been quite helpful, apparently. They've managed to contact a brother in Barcelona, and he's there now. There'll be an autopsy. I also phoned Alfredo just now.'

'Oh?'

'I just wanted to check something . . . Oh, but what does it matter? The damage is done.'

It seemed to Ruth that his mind had drifted to something else. She joined him at the window.

'José?'

'Yes?'

'I'm still frightened.'

She could feel he was ready to go on kissing but resisted, pulling himself away.

'Let's go out for some air,' he said.

16

Ruth smiled to herself as she went to get her coat – the idea of taking walks to talk things over was an English habit José had caught from her. Occasionally, on their way down the narrow street, a burst of drumming struck out at them like a rattlesnake from alleys to left and right. They passed an estate car from which bass drums were being unloaded, their parchment skins paler than the sky. As they began to mount the Monte del Olivo on the far side of town the sound from the main square was a continuum, like the traffic of a city which was not there. Sometimes a gust of wind brought it closer, stumbling as they did up the rocky path, and shook the rows of sapling pines. At their backs the town was a dark island tilted on the hills.

Reaching the summit they passed a group of millstones forming a bed for the tortured olive tree which gave the hill its name; used by picnickers in the summer, José had told her it had been built by republican prisoners doing forced labour after the war. They found shelter on a ledge just below the summit where an outcrop of rocks jutted out over the valley on the town side. Huge convoys of cloud travelled with extreme swiftness over the lowering sky. Yet in the wind's lulls the drums rolled gallantly on, the crepitation of snare-drums shooting out like sparks from the dying embers of a fire.

She sat near him, out of breath, her back to the rock, clutching a piece of fennel she had torn on the way up. Later he turned a little, his face reddened by the wind, his hair swept into different partings.

He said, 'I don't know why you bother with this country.'

She said nothing for a long time, engulfed by a wave of despair: so much of her love was bound up with his hope for the new democracy.

'I love it,' she said faintly.

He tossed a stone he'd picked up far out over the olives.

'And what makes you think it's worth your love?'

The question was unanswerable; besides, she knew it was not so much a question as a challenge.

She said, 'It's you who's always said – who's always believed – that you could overcome the past.'

'Perhaps I'm wrong.'

'Perhaps.'

The wind swooped on the sound like a bird of prey, plucking it from the streets and suddenly releasing it in flight.

She battled on. 'I thought you despised people who gave up just because democracy was more difficult to live with than straight opposition? You've often said how you hate the disenchantment of teenagers, the drug-taking . . .'

'I do hate them – I do. It really makes me angry to see young people taking everything we've fought for for granted. It makes me wonder what I'm working for.'

'Well, if that's how you feel about your work, where does it leave mine? I'm working on something which according to you isn't worth studying –'

'I didn't say that.'

'You implied it when you said you didn't know why I bothered.'

'That wasn't what I meant. Of course, I agree that history's important. I was just suggesting that soon – it's already happening – there are going to be new problems. And setting up a library, working on the anarchist militias – all that will belong to the past.'

'But people will always need history. I wouldn't go on with my work if I didn't think it was relevant . . .'

'All right, then. What relevance does it have?'

Ruth stared out over the valley, as if hoping to find inspiration in the sight of the town where, briefly, the flag of the anarchist federation had hung from the town hall balcony, and the sacked churches had been commandeered as hospitals or warehouses. She didn't resent his question, for it was one she'd often put to herself without being able to find a conclusive answer. Although documentary history was in vogue at the time, Ruth knew she wouldn't be satisfied until she was sure what exactly was the theme behind her work. It was because of an unwillingness to confront this problem except in a vague way that she'd gone on increasing the store of information in the hope that a pattern would emerge.

Still looking down over the town, she allowed her mind to wander over the various reasons which, in the course of her work, had most interested her about the anarchists' experiment. It was true that she had a guarded sympathy for their quixotic idealism, their assumption that by removing the structure of the state they would release people's natural capacity to live with and help each other. She'd been impressed, too, by how some of the collectives were run, at least in the first year of the war. The way one comprehensive ideology came into headlong conflict with another different one – communism – was fascinating, as was the terrifying gulf, in both camps, between theory and practice. There were other possible answers, but none of them addressed the question he'd asked.

'They were people,' she heard herself saying, 'who wanted to improve the world. Whatever terrible things they did – the atrocities they committed, or which were done in their name, still they – or a lot of them at least – were motivated by the ideal of a happier, more integrated society. So much was against them – the war, centuries-long tradition, the communists. But their real failing was not to see that you can't uproot people root and branch from their pasts. Real revolutions happen slowly, and they build on past errors, rather than destroy everything that went before . . .'

She wasn't satisfied by this, yet she felt it contained a seed of what she was searching for.

No answer came. Below them electric lights had come on in some zones of the town; of natural light there only remained a faint glow at the far end of the plain, a twilight over to the south.

There had been a change in José. Ruth could tell it from the way he was sitting, his knees up, his face buried in his arms. How long since he'd stopped listening, she didn't know; it ashamed her that she'd been so absorbed in her thoughts that she'd missed his departure.

She knew this mood as you might recognise a deserted square. It was that *sombra* against which she had no recourse. She remembered the night of her return from the south, when he and Eduardo had been together. Then it had been possible for her to take action; but this was different. It was the barrenness which took him up into the hills. The silence of siesta time. Blank pages of a censored book. The walling-up of Don Quijote's library by the priest and barber who believed that burning the old man's books would make him sane. She was reminded of those moments in her interviews when the words of an interviewee failed. Then an old woman might sit, the tape recording only the sharp buzz of a fly, the flap of a sun curtain on to the concrete street outside, while her own mind would be asking: What? What? – knowing there would be no answer.

And as on those occasions, driving back from the interview, she tried to put herself in the person's shoes, asking herself what was most likely to be troubling him or her at that moment. And suddenly she thought: supposing José had made a wager with himself that Eduardo could be saved?

She reached out and laid her hand over his.

'You can't take his difficulties on your shoulders,' she murmured.

A shake of the head.

'We've got to leave it to the police.'

'I know.'

'Why then –?'

His words stumbled. 'I thought he was worth helping . . .'

He looked up, as if waking from a deep sleep.

'Don't blame yourself. You did what you could – and . . .' The thought came in spite of herself. 'Perhaps he's beyond help?'

He clenched his fist. 'I can't believe that. I can't – I can't.'

'It's because he won't face the past.'

She saw that she'd got through to him: instead of replying he gazed at her for a long time, his face blurred by the darkness.

Suddenly he leaned forwards and kissed her. On another occasion she might have been angry, even hit him for assuming it was all right, but now his kiss answered a need. A breaker of drumming rolled out of the town, withdrawing like a wave.

'Let's go,' she said.

The town was a web of lights on the darkness. Switching on the angle-poise in his room, Ruth waited for him to return from the bathroom. She wanted it to be like the previous night, when they'd sat on his bed and comforted one another; lying there and breathing deeply with her head in his lap, she'd seen the patch of her straw-coloured hair against his black jacket in the wardrobe mirror. Above them on the wall was a poster of Miró's *Birds in the Night*.

She was standing there, recalling this, when he came in still wearing his coat.

'I said I'd go with Elena to talk to our aunt. Do you want to come?'

She shook her head.

'I may stay the night in Belmonte. Oh yes, and . . .' he cleared his throat, 'I'd like to ask you a favour.'

'How formal.'

He said lightly, 'Your small tape-recorder. It's in your room, isn't it? Could I borrow it until tomorrow?'

The request was a sign of forgiveness. Yet, as she went to get the machine and, removing the cassette, replaced it with a new one, she was consumed with curiosity about what he could want it for. As he was leaving she had to ask.

'It's a secret,' he said.

She watched from the window as he strode away from her down the street towards the van.

17

She felt the floor rising and descending as the building unravelled itself over the sound. It was like being on a steamer blundering through high seas, the waves which crashed against its bows leaving long stinging echoes of spray.

Unconsciously, she reached out and leaned against a wall for support.

'José,' she said aloud – but the word was a mere echo of his absence; even if he had been there he could not have heard.

She wandered from room to room, in each of them hearing a different texture of sound against the windows; in one a multiple flicker like hail, in another the thunder of a great wave breaking against the side. The sound crackled in her ears, making unexpected deflections off the ceilings and tiled floor.

Lying down on the living-room divan, she closed her eyes. Floating lights rose and sank behind her eyelids like flares over the sea. She opened them and the room was unchanged, occupied by the ghosts of the drums. Their bones rattled as they danced, and the long veils of sound undulated through the flat's walls, bringing in the damp ozone-scented air of the land. Her limbs detached themselves and began to dance with the phantoms of sound.

Suddenly she realised that the flat was dead and life was below in the streets and square, an inexplicable pandemonium bewitching the whole land. She felt the overwhelming strength of it, the undertow of a wave dragging her through the flat like a piece of flotsam, barely giving her time to slam down the blinds, find her coat, keys, money – before she plummeted down the chasm of the stairs.

Most of the drummers had already dispersed from the *plaza* where the *rompida* had taken place, but a few still remained, their rhythm dissolving into one another as she hurried across the square. Descending the Calle Mayor she heard the boom of the cataract above. When she reached the workshop beyond the bridge she was relieved to see a light in the window above the door, casting a faint glimmer into the mist above the muddy yard.

Four people were inside, drinking red wine or cola from paper cups; although a fan-heater was roaring their breaths were visible on the air. Pedro came forward with a smile to introduce her to a girl of thirteen or so with a brace on her teeth; Ruth already knew her sister, a plump girl who served in his family's cake shop. Finally, Luis got down from the desk on which he was perched and came over, very grown-up, to give her his hand.

Pedro ragged Ruth about the lost car; but as soon as she put down her cup they set off, Pedro next to the cake-girl who was driving, Ruth sitting in the back seat with Luis and the younger girl. There was a sugar-taste of cheap scent; a new bass drum bounced on Luis's knees.

'Did your father give you that?' Ruth asked; but Luis did not reply, unmanned by the proximity of a girl of his own age.

The wine had warmed the three adults; they were in such high spirits that the cake-girl began singing *jotas* as she drove; soon her sister joined in. 'To dance the *jota* . . .' they chanted. 'The requirements are these . . . To be from Aragón, and to be Aragonese . . .' Later they goaded Pedro until he shouted in a hoarse voice: 'The girl I love . . . Has dark brown hair. Only the Virgin of the Pilar . . . is more lovely and fair . . .'

'Well?' the cake-girl yelled over her shoulder. 'What do you think of our *jota* demonstration? Do we get the prize?' As they drove towards Calanda they entered a region of fog, which slowed them down; the red lights of cars ahead became mysterious before

137

vanishing completely. When they got out of the car the drums' clamour was already audible, though muffled by the wet air.

They locked the car and began to move towards the square with the stream of people. This mist was penetrating: Ruth tucked her scarf in tightly to protect her throat. She felt as if she had left the trauma of the last few days behind and abandoned herself to the current of people which meandered between cars and shuttered shops; she felt free and a little reckless, like a teenager going to a party.

She knew Calanda from having done a number of interviews there, and from a visit to Teresa's family with José. It was a fruit and wheat-rich village on the plain, several small new blocks standing on a street leading to the centre of town; a place of more than usual ordinariness. But tonight, in the mist and darkness, it was like a stage-set seen from behind in a darkened theatre, its walls drained of colour by the white spill of street-lamps.

Suddenly a brash glare of noise flashed out and a group of drummers appeared, stalking down the street towards them. Long purple satin tunics. Surgeons caps with stepped tongues at the back. Small banners hung on their drums with the symbol of the church guild they belonged to – the tools of Christ's torture. The eyes of the people they passed were bright with animation. In their wake a woman ran, carrying a *bombo* like a suitcase, her fingers through its cords, and a toddler bounced along on her father's shoulders, whacking a toy drum. As she walked between metal frames fixed across the street at intervals to stop cars, Ruth felt the first breath of the sound from the square on her cheeks.

At the corner of a street the buzzing of a resistor made her look up. A cat's cradle of wires gathered and twisted around a bracket above a shop's illuminated sign. By the wall they were pale from the sign below; farther up the street they darkened, threading the mist. She passed through the smoke from a *churros* maker's and the brightness of a row of stalls selling garish tubes of sweets. Then the street turned abruptly; it was as if a door had fallen open, letting the sound through. The entrance to the *plaza* ahead was filled with purple figures, the blur of drumsticks against their chests. The drums were a choppy sea of pale discs in the glare of a floodlight.

The sound had changed. There were two strands of it now – the meretricious shatter straight ahead and a deep growl, like the premonition of an earthquake, from the square beyond. She left Pedro and the others watching the guild playing in its mouth and found herself in an arcade on one side of the square. She could understand why no one lingered there: the place snatched the sound, tossing it up to a beamed ceiling from which it fell with a hollow rattle like bullets perforating a metal sheet. Stepping out of the arcade, she began to push into the body of the crowd until the mass of drummers all around blocked her progress completely.

She was surrounded by satin backs crossed with leather straps, rolled-up sleeves thumping huge *bombos,* the rattle of sticks on transparent skins, while in the middle-distance the clubs rose and for a split-second seemed to hang above the crowd – so many bean-bags tossed high into the air. Some drummers looked down, as if their whole body were absorbed in the action of drumming; others were on the alert for a change in rhythm by their leader – boys anxious to make a good impression on their first admission to a guild. There was a young woman with a dead face staring out into the noise as if into a high wind, her mind distant from the rhythm flowing from her arms. Some of them appeared riveted by the opiate of the drums. A flabby-faced man had a look of triumph, his brow glistening with sweat, released by the action of drumming into an ecstatic trance. And there were drummers in dark glasses, their identities masked like penitents in pointed hoods – and in the same way the effect was sinister, especially when you glimpsed another square, its toy drums flickering in the dark shields.

From a distance the sound's solidity made it the exact counterpart of silence. In adjusting to it Ruth found that her ears would sometimes give up so that she could hear nothing; a moment later it would return with redoubled force. As her eardrums contracted they altered its density, crumbling it into small fragments of rhythm which tumbled down on to one another, burying some and exposing others. Sometimes her ears were a microscope, focusing on a minute texture like the scratched surface of a wall; suddenly, without warning, they would take in the whole spectrum of sound flooding the wide square and spreading out into the shrouded land beyond.

Ruth was glad she had come – she was smiling, but she did not know why she was glad. Was it because of the absolute reality of the drums? The way they combined everybody in a single activity? Or their hard, unmitigated energy? They were no more than themselves, posing no questions, offering no answers. Yet it seemed to her that they embodied the spirit of everything.

'The spirit of everything' – the phrase was too solemn, for the drums had also released her from herself, making her laugh out loud. They were comic – perhaps this was because they gathered so many people together in a communal action which, strictly speaking, was unnecessary. Yet they felt essential to the human body, spirit – everything. They brought life – and death, too, for their purpose was to send it packing – into focus. And they were not, like many spiritual exercises, a means to solitary revelation; they embraced everyone, while – a true anarchist, Ruth thought, would have approved – honouring the contribution of every individual.

They were a practice, not a theory. They called bread, bread and wine, wine. Only they called nothing anything, for their medium was not words, nor thoughts, either, but the human beings who played them. She remembered José's words about them destroying time. Had he meant that, because they took place every year, each ceremony contained the trace of the previous ones? The drums were layered, like history.

After a while people began to move and disperse at the edges of the square, causing the sound to spread and mingle as it flowed out into the streets. Many of the remaining groups were competing, trying to impose their rhythms on others by playing more loudly so that their opponents would either falter because they could no longer hear one another, or depart to seek fresh antagonists. As she wended her way through the crowd the ground trembled and shifted beneath her feet so that she felt as if she were walking on stepping-stones of sound, striding precariously from one to another as they bulged and slid until, reaching the arcade, she had to prop herself against a wooden pillar which imparted a rhythm of its own.

Looking back for a moment into the darkness of the arcade, she saw a pair of doors open and a little girl come out on the hand of a tall blonde woman. As the two of them passed the lighted window of a bar the little girl looked over her shoulder, and she recognised Alicia, the sculptor's daughter. Was that her mother with her? Perhaps they lived here. They had left one of the doors slightly ajar. Out of curiosity, but also tempted by the chance of a respite from the sound's onslaught, Ruth entered and began to mount a tiled flight of stairs. A mustiness in the air suggested the building was unused.

In a room on the first floor a couple of trestle tables with a lot of paper cups on them and a full ash-tray stood against a wall. A clapper-board lay on a tattered leather chair. By the light of a single bulb a man and a woman sat, bending over a large tape-recorder; the balcony windows were closed to allow them to check the recording. It took her some time to realise that this too was of the drums: the taped version spread its skein over the actual drums in the square below. The woman looked up, but made no sign.

What had Alicia been doing up here? Then she knew – she had remembered the pile of film equipment up at her father's house and his dismissive attitude to the film crew. The sound cracked open: they had switched off the machine and opened a window; now the woman and her companion were sidling through it to stand out on the balcony, smoking over the rail. Ruth slipped out behind them.

The sound attacked her, shooting off the skins of the drums and glancing from house to house around the arena of the square; she felt a sudden dizziness, as if from the change of pressure in a descending plane. In one long gaze she took in the town hall with its illuminated clock and balconies draped with the Spanish and Aragonese flags, the church with its empty niche above the porch, the crowded balconies of the houses on the left side of the square. Among the mass of satin shoulders and dark heads the drums were scattered like coins at the bottom of a well.

After a while she spotted Alfredo – a frenzy of disordered white hair and sleeveless arms – drumming in a splash of light. Two cameras were on him, dark insects balanced on men's shoulders in the brightness of the lamps. It was easy to imagine the picture as it would appear on screen: the bearded man with his arms blurred amidst the turmoil of drums. She was thinking of Eduardo – why had things worked out so much better for his friend the sculptor? They were contemporaries, after all – when she saw a man with swept-back hair standing over towards the Banco Central.

Something about him made her look again. It was the hair that was familiar, the way its edge formed a bow-shape on the brow. He was wearing mirrored glasses. No drum. A needle of fear pricked her neck. Was it Eduardo's pursuer? Where was his driver? She searched again, but in the swirling wake caused by the penetration of a new guild into the square, the man she'd seen had turned his head. There was no sign of the younger man.

She tried to focus her eyes on the patch of crowd where she'd glimpsed the hair, but the sound itself seemed to blurr her vision; she could see nothing. If it were them, she thought, she should do some- thing – tell the police. Leaving the balcony, she went out and down the stairs and began to push her way towards the centre of the crowd.

Before she could get there a heavy hand seized her shoulder. It was Pedro, giving her a broad smile, while around them she suddenly recognised Luis and the two girls, all drumming. Pedro had stopped and nodded to his girlfriend, who at once unshouldered her drum and lassooed Ruth's neck with the strap. She could feel her mouth yelling 'No! Listen! Not now!' as the leather strap bit the graze on her shoulder. But Pedro had not noticed her protest, and the cake- girl had already turned her back and was bobbing away through the crowd. The leather thong of the thick club had slid over her wrist.

Ruth felt helpless, the great burden sticking out in front of her. There was no sign of the man she had seen – or thought she'd seen – from the balcony. She felt almost certain now that she'd imagined him; there had been no sign of his companion; besides, even if she had not been mistaken, what could she do? An answer came: 'Call Elena' – but she might be out, and it would be complicated to explain to the police. The argument of the drums was overwhelming. Already her hand was grasping the polished wooden handle while the other swept over the parchment in front of her, feeling the slight roughness at its edges and the smoothness of the centre where it was slacker by a few millimetres. She cupped the thick club in her hand, rubbing the leather laces which bound it to the stick. She tried bouncing it gently on the skin and felt the first deep thump in her, a baby's heart. She felt herself blushing as the girl with the brace caught her eye and smiled.

Pedro edged his way through to her, the sticks of his side-drum crushed against his chest. He arranged them and nodded to her and Luis; then started with a flourish. His part, the side-drum part, was far more complex and intricate than the slower rhythm which she and the other *bombo* players were to supply.

She could hear two rhythms in that part of the square – a slow pounding one, repeated several times before it sped up in a sudden wild crescendo and then dipped back into the pounding again, and a faster, more syncopated rhythm to their left. The one on the right felt closer. Luis and his brother were doing this. When his brother got it right, Pedro did nothing; it was the same when he made a slip, for it was obvious from the sound. Luckily, the pattern was one of the simplest, involving counting more than a sense of rhythm. 'Short, short – long,' the *bombos* went. 'Short, short – long. Short, short, short, short, short, short – long.' Once again. Then, getting louder: 'Short, short, short, short; short, short, short, short; short, short, short, short – long, long.' This last passage – the crescendo – seemed as if it would continue forever on its hectic career until the beats' number was up and the first 'short, short – longs' began again.

She started to do the first section, waiting, then joining in when it came round again. As she drummed, she felt the weight of the sound in her body, the unfamiliar strain in her arm right through to her shoulder-blade. She smiled at Luis, enjoying this first success. Then she tried the second section. The accelerating run of strokes had its own momentum. She was doing it now, too, and Pedro turned away from both her and Luis, signalling the end of their initiation. She still made mistakes, missing beats, beating on the upbeat, forgetting to count so that she inserted a long beat into the run of short ones, but no one minded. A stray stroke would either be absorbed – or, by chance, it would fit into another pattern which was only yards away.

She was pleased now, glad that Luis watched her sometimes, so she led them both. Then her eyes focused on the movements of the drummers in a circle beyond as their clubs floated, paused above their heads before swooping to a different beat, and the sight made her go wrong. Luis had managed to drum on. So now she followed the boy, and this time the rhythm was familiar, like a well-worn pair of shoes.

And then it happened: the event which, without knowing it, she had desired all along. Not for a long time, at first, but for a few seconds before another thought made her arm forget and she had to apply herself again, the drum began to drum itself without her consciously willing it, the sound rocketing out of her arm, shoulder, body. It had taken flight from her mind. Suddenly everything around – the juddering square, the flights of clubs leaping above heads, the looks exchanged around the group – was woven into a single cloth. She was no longer alone in the island of her faults and virtues; she was part of a conglomerate action in which, having lost herself, she expanded to include the whole flickering madness of the town stretching right out on to the plain. Yet the sensation was not frightening because she had drummed herself into this state, could walk away and see herself in it, separate before returning. The sound splashed and dissolved her as the sea degrades rock and then dredges it up, a myriad of pebbles, on the shore.

The sensation lasted only a moment. Then Luis had gone; smoke was blowing into her face from a fag end clenched in the mouth of the drummer next to her; a slight breeze bulged the striped flags draped over a balcony.

When her arm got tired she stopped drumming and began to wander, counting four or five different rhythms being played in the square. One was solid and rigorous until it was interrupted by a sudden hiatus, a withdrawal of energy; another, in spite of its rapidity, had an elegiac quality. Sometimes she heard the echo of one figure inside another, unable to tell if it were her memory or the drums themselves playing a trick. Stubbornly, her mind would batten on to one pattern while the players near her were executing another. And she felt the disorientation of standing between two rhythms, hearing the friction between them in which every beat was wrong.

Seeing the pale disc of the church clock, she had an image of the groups around her as many clocks running at different speeds whose hours sometimes coincided, defining a fluid geography whose frontiers wavered and overlapped.

She left the square, but not the sound, for in the sparsely lighted streets it danced, snapping at her from eaves, or growling in the distance, hushed by mist. The footsteps of a little girl slapped on the concrete road as she ran past excitedly, her drum swinging on her back. In one street, defined only by a cone of light in the foggy air, the houses looked dead, their souls gone to the square.

She had forgotten the sound, grown used to it as you might a sort of weather, when she was suddenly deafened by a group of boys laying claim to the street ahead. She followed them into a confluence of streets where twenty or thirty more drummers were gathered beneath a saint's statue in a glazed niche above an arch. She peered over the shoulders of a man in a grey anorak to where, at the centre of the group, a tiny muscular man was smashing the life out of a sidedrum while his eyes flashed out approval or tolerance at the work of the players around him.

The man in front of her turned his head. She just had time to see the bruised pallor, the smudge of the moustache, and to smell the alcohol on his breath.

'Eduardo!' she blurted.

'Leave me alone,' he said. He was striding away from her, without looking back, in the direction of the arch. But she knew she had to warn him.

'Eduardo! Come back! They're here!'

She pushed her way through the crowd under the arch to where, on the far side, another posse of drummers in dark glasses were plunging down towards her. As she flattened herself against the wall to let them pass she was sure she saw a glimpse of Eduardo's silver-streaked hair, the hunch of his back. She ran on, but so did the street, extending ahead of her into the mist.

18

The drummers had dispersed into side-streets, staking out the whole town. Figures crossed her path as she ran, the sound leaping like a wild animal to snap at her legs or clinging like cobwebs to her face. Once, passing a dark shape, she had the distinct sensation that it was drumming silently and that the noise was coming from the far side of the street where mist unfurled in the light of a lamp. Other shapes sat on door-steps, their arms around each other; and from the depths of a lane came the clang of an oil-drum being banged in an eccentric solitary rhythm.

The damp air tickled her brow. She began to think what she was doing, and her pace slackened to a walk. She had at first had no other idea than to warn Eduardo of the danger he might be facing; now she realised that the last thing she wanted was to be surprised by him in an alley, let alone by his pursuers – if indeed she had seen one of them. Various options occurred to her. Should she go to the police? Should she try to get in touch with Elena? Perhaps José would still be there, or the two of them might have gone to his parents' house in Belmonte.

Some way ahead the form of a man brushed a cone of light and vanished in the darkness.

She looked back, but no one was following. She began to walk after the figure very slowly, trying to keep it just in sight before it was swallowed by the mist. She was not sure it was Eduardo, though the shape she had seen might have been of a long anorak. It would be all right to go on, she decided, as long as she kept well back and made sure there was no one behind. At a distance, the noise was diminished, like a memory of the sea; it was a relief to be out of it. The drum hindered her progress.

The drum . . . She remembered Pedro and the arrangement they had made to meet in the bar on the square at half past twelve. She stopped to check her watch under a lamp – it was a quarter to; when she looked up the figure ahead had also paused in a pool of light and seemed to be hesitating. Then it proceeded into the thick night. She followed, into a wider street where a cold wind told her she had reached the edge of the town. Its freezing dankness enveloped her face, full of the land's odours and the stink of manure.

Suddenly a bulb came on in a doorway in one of the houses to her left, and she was close enough to catch sight of a man's face as he turned, waiting to be let in. He was clean-shaven, wearing a bomber jacket, not an anorak. Some female voices cheered as the door opened, then the light beyond the door was shut in. It had not been Eduardo at all.

She realised that she was at the foot of a *calvario*, one of those small hills with a hermitage at its crest just outside a town. Giving up all thoughts of finding Eduardo, she decided to get to the top: the very short walk would give her a rest from the racket of the drums and a chance to disentangle speculation from what she'd really seen.

She was sure Eduardo had been there. Alfredo, too – though this surprised her because she'd assumed that that was whom José would go to talk to after meeting Elena. But the two men – she might have seen one of them, or she might not, before having the drum thrust into her hands.

By the spill of light from the town, she could tell that she was almost at the top. An icy trickle of mud pricked through her socks: at some point she must have missed the path. Below her she could make out a threshing-floor near which a group of mill-stones leaned against each other in stolid companionship. A night bird emitted a harsh, feral call, its wings pothering after. There were no yews to keep vigil about the new brick hermitage which dominated the hill, only the last of the stations of the cross – concrete pillars supporting an empty shelf like a garden letter-box – which had helped to guide her up.

The lights of the village lit certain roofs and angles above the mist, while the occasional pair of headlamps swept out to the right. The extent of Calanda was defined by the faint grumble of drums. Sometimes, when a guild passed a certain juxtaposition of houses, a whiplash struck out into the silence of the land.

Something made her head turn. Was it a sound-memory – an echo of what her ears had suffered earlier, or was the breeze really carrying across the plain, on the back of the mist, the noise of drumming in the next town twelve kilometres along the road? Before she could decide if this were true a flash of lightning – then another – burst open a violet cloud cave far out above the hills. Its thunderclap obliterated the drums.

Suddenly she knew what to do: Teresa's parents lived in the village. She didn't want to go straight to the police because she dreaded having to explain everything on her own; nor did she wish to ring José's family house in Belmonte and risk worrying his mother if he were not there. Besides, there was a chance that Elena might be with Teresa, and they could go to the police together. She was troubled by only one doubt as she descended the slope: the thought that it might be better not to disturb Eduardo's wife – she was likely to be upset enough as it was. But, putting herself in Teresa's shoes, Ruth decided that she would not want to have anything concealed from her.

The street was so wide, with the small hedged garden in the centre, that the far side was barely visible through the mist. She gauged which she thought the house was and rang a couple of door-bells, but got no reply. Then she decided that her memory had reversed the street, and she went round the garden to the other side.

An instant later the very overweight person of Teresa's mother came to the door in a knitted cardigan. Ruth was given no chance of explaining the situation discreetly without at once bothering Teresa; no sooner had she seen her than the woman was shouting in a deafening voice: 'Tere! It's the English girl!' Then she said kindly, 'Go through, my dear.'

Ruth left her drum in the kitchen and, as the woman indicated, went through into a barely furnished room which appeared to have once been a small boy's bedroom: there were posters of motorbikes on the walls and model warplanes suspended by threads from the ceiling. Teresa rose from a chair.

'You say he's here – in Calanda?'

'Yes – I even tried to follow him for a while, but I lost him. And also . . .' Ruth hesitated, wondering if it were right to mention this. 'I think I may have seen one of the men who were following him.'

She regretted the remark at once. Poor Teresa looked at the end of her tether, standing there like one of her own patients in a padded dressing-gown too large for her, a pile of knitting discarded on the bed. Ruth had seen how wretched she was, yet she had reckoned – wrongly, she now thought – that she had a responsibility to mention what she might have seen. If only she had gone herself to the police station.

But Teresa had moved to the doorway to consult rapidly with her mother in Spanish; they were talking about the police. Ruth rose, feeling guilty, and interjected: 'I definitely saw him, but about the others I can't be sure.'

'My mother will phone them.'

'José was given a special number to ring, but I didn't take it . . . I thought he might be here.'

Teresa said again, 'My mother will phone them.'

Her hand touched Ruth's shoulder as they returned into the room; Ruth felt a combination of relief at the fact that someone was coping and a sense of the absurdity of Teresa's reassuring her.

'Listen – I'm sorry, Teresa. Perhaps I shouldn't have come. I'm sorry . . .'

'It's all right. I'm glad.' She indicated the bed. 'Did you come to hear the drums?'

Ruth nodded.

'You were right to come to the drums. And you say you've seen him? In Calanda?'

'Mm. Perhaps –' she was about to say he might come here, but she stopped herself.

Teresa said, 'He may be all right, then. You know he telephoned me, don't you?'

'No.'

'It was this morning, at about seven. My mother woke me up. He said . . .' she was bandaging her hand with a napkin which she'd taken from a tray with an empty cup and a sachet of coffee on it lying on the desk. 'He said nothing for a long time, and then I said, "What have you done, man?" He didn't reply. He just said, "You've got nothing to do with this, Tere." There was this long silence and he hung up. And then . . . perhaps it was him, because a couple of hours ago the door-bell rang, and when we went down there was no one. We thought it was some boys playing a game . . .' Her tired eyes met Ruth's.

'Perhaps he wanted to make it up to you and didn't know how.'

'But why doesn't he know? Why?'

Ruth said nothing.

'It was the same before, when those men were phoning him. If only he'd spoken to me about it before. Perhaps I couldn't have helped, but at least . . . at least we'd have been sharing.'

'Yes.'

'And now – Elena told me – he may have killed someone. But you know I still care about him, Ruth. Maybe I'm wrong, but I know somewhere inside him he's all right. It's just – it's got lost . . .'

She flung away the napkin with a look of disgust. Her face was expressionless, yet Ruth felt she understood the battle she was fighting to get herself back from this man who no longer needed her.

Then Teresa's eyes came to rest on a picture-postcard which was lying beside the tray: a night view of the Eiffel Tower. She picked it up, saying, 'Do you know why I think he's all right? Once, when we were going out – we were very happy, or I thought we were – we went

151

to Paris for a weekend, and when we came back, he said he was leaving me . . . I didn't see him again for months, though he did telephone sometimes. I thought, well, maybe he's got another woman or something, but do you know what it was?'

Ruth shook her head.

'He can't have children.' Somehow the sad phrase accorded with her blotchy face, the heap of knitting, the tray by the bed. She went on, 'It was almost by chance that I found out. I'd bumped into him one evening, and you know how it is – it was then that he told me. And that was the reason he wasn't seeing me. Because he knew I'd want to get married and it was a question he didn't want me to have to ask myself. I told him I didn't mind.'

'Didn't you?'

'I wouldn't have if . . . if things had gone all right. But then this began . . . oh, and there had been so many problems before . . .'

As Teresa went on turning the postcard over in her hands, Ruth tried to imagine what had caused her to become a nurse. The death of a member of her family, perhaps? The patient who mattered to her most seemed to have proved incurable, and Ruth couldn't help asking herself if she would have enough energy left to nurse herself.

Suddenly rising from the bed, she put her arms round her and kissed her on the cheek. Feeling the pounding of her heart – or was it Teresa's? – she wondered what had stripped her of the inhibitions which usually prevented her from sharing herself. The postcard had slipped on to the floor.

They were interrupted by her mother coming in to say that the police had called back and wanted to speak to Teresa. The plump woman encouraged Ruth to stay the night but, although it was late, she decided to try to find the others in the square: she wanted to return to Alcañiz. Kissing the two women good-bye, she stepped out into the sting of drums and air.

19

The imprint of Teresa's kisses on her cheeks had worn off by the time Ruth entered the *plaza* again, but the warmth of their conversation glowed inside her; she felt she'd been able to comfort her a little. And, crossing the square with the *bombo* over her shoulder, she realised she associated this feeling with that moment when her arm had begun to beat the drum of its own accord.

The mood of the ceremony had changed. The storm Ruth had seen over the hills had not reached Calanda yet, but the air was dense with its impending arrival. It changed the sound, too, suffocating it so that the pulse of bass drums was like the throbbing of a vein in the forehead. Now only the most committed drummers remained, gathered in knots under the lamps, determined to keep at it all night, however hard it might be. Some had knuckles brushed with blood from the battering they were giving them: it was impossible to beat a *bombo* without grazing the edge of the hand on the drumhead and, after a while, spattering the parchment, refreshing the stains of previous years.

There was no sign of Pedro or the others in the porch of the church. It was her fault – the town hall clock read twenty to one. She decided to check the interior – they might have wanted to sit down – before going back to Teresa's parents' house to spend the night.

The church was brighter than she'd expected, its light enhanced by stucco walls, a polished floor. Lingering by the conch, she heard the dabble of fingers before an old lady crossed herself, genuflecting

153

to the altar. Over to her left a velvet-skirted float – its image shrouded in purple – stood in readiness for the street procession the next day. Stacked behind it was a panel pinned with photographs of a mission farm in Africa: a child proffering a gourd; a herd of emaciated cattle; a man leaning on a stick. In the midst of these was a large painting – clearly done by a whole class of children – of Noah's ark. Brightly coloured animals progressed two by two up a gangplank, or leaned their heads over the rail, presided over by a tall Noah with a cotton-wool beard.

The sound raged on outside. Even now, when the drums were no longer at full spate, the high windows were in a crossfire while the church walls resounded with a boom of artillery. It felt as if, at any moment, the roof was about to crash down and bury the congregation in a heap of rubble.

Perhaps it was the sight of blood on the parchment, but a hoard of images thronged into Ruth's head, and this time they were the worst: a cascade of bombs tumbling down on to a port; a bound man recoiling and crumpling on a chair; the blank terror of a group of prisoners forced to watch their comrades slaughtered in a mock bullfight . . .

A low muttering rose and sank beneath the surface of the noise. It was a group of women, hunched over their rosaries, notching up Ave Marias; beyond them on the altar steps a priest chatted to a man kneading a black beret in his hands. Shoes squeaked and shuffled on the floor.

Ruth left the *bombo* on a chair and walked down the nave to a side chapel in which four wax figures were standing at the corners of a glass catafalque. They were dressed as Roman soldiers, in red tunics, brass greaves and breast-plates, leather sandals, and armed with swords and spears. She caught an eye-movement – one of them had come alive; then the four young men were still again, keeping vigil over the glass case.

The body of Christ did not move. It was pillowed on a velvet cushion; through the reflection of a guttering candle she saw the glimpse of a yellow plaster face, the rest of the body shrouded in white linen. It had occurred to her that the shroud was a reminder of the baby Jesus's swaddling clothes when a heavily-built man moved out of the row of chairs just behind where she stood and began to travel away from her down the church.

She knew at once it was Eduardo. The broad shoulders, the fraying anorak, the dishevelled hair . . . He was making unsteady progress down the aisle.

She had taken a few paces after him when she saw him stop and hesitate by one of the stations of the cross on the wall. He was rocking a little forwards and back, as if tracing the steps of a dance known only to himself. Drunk, of course.

The two men must have come in, as he had, by the north entrance, for they were standing by the wooden box over the doors. The driver with the squarish face. His shorter companion with the swept-back hair and the slightly protruding area of flesh around the mouth. The sticking-plaster was gone from his brow, but he had his hands in the pockets of his mackintosh as before. Both of them were staring at Eduardo across the lines of chairs.

Suddenly Ruth went up to him and, taking him firmly by the arm, began to steer him rapidly out of the church by the south door. She didn't stop to ask herself what was driving her, whether the half-remembered image of the tramp in Granada, or the knowledge of Teresa's love, or the sense that this was a chance to transcend the confines of her work. Nor did she think of the consequences. She was only conscious of something inside crying out to her to save Eduardo, not from the process of the law but from the men who were hounding him. All of a sudden it was clear to her that his well-being was bound up with her own. But, as the drunken man turned towards her on the steps, recognition dawning in his eyes, his breath foul with alcohol, she was assaulted by a rising panic at the thought of what she was doing. Possibly he sensed this through the fog of brandy, for he mumbled, 'Leave me, *inglesa* . . . ' But he was gripping her arm.

She tried to think. Leave him – he was right. But where? Out of danger, if possible – somewhere where the police could find him. Should she try to get him to Teresa's? But that was on the other side of the church, and the two men . . .

There was a bar on the other side of the street. If she could take him in there, sit him down – even if it had to be with a drink, and then use the phone . . . She looked back anxiously as she almost pulled him across the road, but there was no sign of his two pursuers on the church steps.

The air of the bar was steamy with the sweat of resting drummers. All the tables were full: she had to go up to a red-faced woman in a tunic and ask if she could extract a chair. Luckily, when she brought it for Eduardo he slumped down immediately, mesmerised by a float in a Holy Week procession in the south – Christ praying in the garden – which was staggering across the screen of the bar's television.

As she waited for the waiter to pass her the telephone she glanced out of the window with unease. It was difficult to be sure, through the forest of drinkers near the bar, but the church door seemed to be closed. She remembered she had left the drum inside – God knows what Pedro would say. It wasn't until the phone had appeared on the counter that she realised she did not know Teresa's family name, let alone their number.

A gap opened in the crowd. Eduardo's chair was empty: she was just in time to see the anorak's long back disappearing through a door just behind her.

The two men were standing in the entrance to the bar. She was pretty certain they had not seen her – the older one, at least, was still surveying the tables as she slipped out after Eduardo, her heart pounding. To her side a doorway led into a large room with a rock band's equipment on a dais. Empty. She tried another way down the corridor through a pair of doors which led into what looked like a cinema foyer. The street entrance was closed.

She was not sure how much she wanted to find Eduardo now. Since her impulse in the church she'd come to recognise more clearly the danger she was running. She told herself: He's a murderer, and as she searched for a way out – passing through two more doors, she found herself in the cinema itself – she no longer knew if she were going after him or simply trying to escape. Vaguely aware of an old man with a bunch of keys shouting and gesticulating at her from a block of seats, she ran past him into another corridor and at last the street.

The car leaped out of darkness, suddenly rising and hurtling towards her; she jumped sideways just in time, hearing the wheels slam against the kerb. Then it lay helplessly across the pavement, a headlight which had crunched into the wall tinkling to the ground. It had been driven without lights. Her first reaction was anger – she could have been maimed or killed, and she was just about to go up to the car and berate the driver when she saw who it was.

Somehow Eduardo had managed to get his car going – but not to aim it along the street. He must have been trying to get out of town, but in the state he was in he was as likely to kill himself as to die at the hands of the two men.

The deserted jeep was parked just down the street on the other side. Seeing this, Ruth abandoned her initial plan to ring the bell of one of the houses and ask for help. As Eduardo wound down the window she began to shout at him to heave himself over on to the passenger seat and give her the key. She felt a kind of exhilaration as she turned on the ignition and the unfamiliar car sprang to life beneath her hands. But, stalling and jerking forwards down the narrow street, her fear returned so that the sally of a drum out of a lane made her almost leap out of the seat. Her fingers were trembling on the wheel. She checked the mirror, but to her relief the jeep was still parked behind them.

She forced herself to think slowly, giving enough time to each option to be able to consider it objectively. One was to take Eduardo straight to the *guardia* while he was still drunk enough hardly to know what was happening, but she didn't know which side of Calanda that was on – and there was a risk that in trying to find it the men might catch up. Another was to find a public telephone, but not

157

knowing the police's number would delay her, and meanwhile she would have abandoned him in the car. Finally, she could just keep driving on out of town, putting as much distance as possible between them and the pursuers, the objection to this being that Eduardo might sober up and become intractable – even dangerous.

She was on the verge of despair – none of these courses of action seemed right – when she caught sight of a sign indicating the road to Belmonte. Suddenly she made a decision: she would leave him in the old house in the village, and then go as quickly as possible to José's parents' house – they would alert the police. Her relief at having hit on a plan translated itself into a single aim: to drive fast to Belmonte, where, out of range of the two men, Eduardo could be handed over to the authorities.

They were outside the town now, rain teeming in the lopsided glare of the working headlight. The sight of a beam of light in the mirror turned her neck into a pin-cushion – then it swung off on to a path and she realised it had been a motorbike. She was aware of a stench of alcohol in the car blended with sweat. Its source sat in silence, apparently unaware of her anxiety. There was an ear-rending crack of thunder as they entered the storm; then a shaft of blackness lunged up at them, and she had to swerve to avoid plummeting into a stretch of the reservoir.

She was glad Eduardo wasn't behind her. Glancing to her right, she tried to gauge the state he was in, but it was so dark in the car, except for the odd spasm of lightning, that all she could see was the shape of his head as he gazed out at the darkness brimming below the road. The sight of the pale hand on his knee caused the word 'murderer' to creep again into her mind, and with it a series of questions: Who had the dead man been? Where had Eduardo been since? Was he still armed? She was distracted by an oncoming car, forcing her to crawl into the side furthest from the water while it edged past inch by inch. Then they were alone again, wipers creaking as the road snaked up into the sierra.

There was a sudden violent increase of rain and the road had vanished, the lamp's beam swallowed by mist and darkness. The only thing to do was to bring the car to a standstill. As long as any other traffic would do the same.

As soon as the car stopped, she heard a click: her passenger had opened the door and was staggering out into the night. A short time before she might have cared – even gone after him, but just now a feeling of helplessness came over her. She supposed from his posture that he was urinating into the rain. Wind buffeted the car. She was conscious of aches in her body, the soreness from the drum-strap; tiredness circumscribed her eyes. The Spanish word for 'nothing' – *nada* – teased her lips: the word itself sounded void of meaning. Waiting in that relentless battering darkness, she realised she was too tired to think about the crime he had committed.

Then he was beside her again, drenched and out of breath.

'Eduardo,' she murmured, 'who are those men?'

She had almost forgotten asking the question by the time he grunted and said heavily, 'The old man's nephew.'

Rain thrashed on the roof. He had turned his face just a little so that, by the faint glow of the dashboard, she could see the outline of his cheek.

'You know, José and I . . .' She swallowed. 'We went to visit Alfredo . . .'

'Alfredo Ariño?'

'Yes.'

The volume of noise in the car – the hammering of rain competing with the rattle of the heater – meant that she had to ask him to repeat his question – 'What for?'

'We'd had an accident. But then, José . . . José . . .' She took a deep breath. 'It isn't true, is it, that you worked for the police?'

A sudden draught made her shiver. Then Eduardo turned away, so that all she could see was the shape of his dishevelled hair as he stared out into the night.

Finally he said, 'Did Alfredo tell you that?'

'No. We – that is, José . . . He guessed.'

'So . . . José knows everything?'

'No . . . At least – I don't think so. I don't . . .' Her face burned, though it was cold in the car. She said, 'Then he was right?'

He produced a sound which might have been a belch. In the long silence which ensued it seemed to her that she could imagine the early part of his story without his saying a word: she hadn't realised how much work her imagination had done over the last few days. Of course, it was no more than a fiction founded on the little she knew; yet now it was almost as if the darkness were a screen on which fragments of a film about him were playing soundlessly.

She imagined him joining the party as a young man, partly out of conviction and partly because it was forbidden, a continuation of the secret societies he had known as a boy: children meeting by candle-light behind a garage door. She envisaged the motion of a press in an underground cellar; a pair of civil guards passing along the corridor of a train; leaflets being removed from inside the seat of a car. She saw him with dark glasses and sideburns distributing propaganda at the entrance to a lecture hall, an image suddenly obscured by clouds of tear-gas through which, batons raised, the police charged on horse-back. She was with him in the back of a police van hurtling to brigade headquarters, and beside him when he recognised the officer doodling on a blotter as his father's friend. Night after night he paced the rooms of a flat while his student friends slept behind closed doors. At a clandestine party meeting she watched him playing listlessly with a pencil as the men around him debated fiercely through a veil of cigarette smoke. And she spied on him from a balcony on the far side of the street when, in an unfurnished attic, he was presented with a list of names, a set of photographs, before – it was evening when he left the building – a tall pillar cast by the setting sun caught him buying a sheet of lottery tickets from a blind salesman in the porch below.

All this ran through her head, so it was almost as if he'd been speaking and she needed to confirm something when she said, 'The old man . . . He was your *jefe* . . . In the police, I mean?'

His reply was lost in the detonation of a thunderclap. In the brief twilight injected into that waterscape the rain had started to clear: she saw the ghost of an olive tree, with the outline of a sign beneath. When the second flash came the word 'Belmonte' blazed and recoiled on her retina. For the last ten minutes or so they had been sitting at the edge of the village.

'We're going to the old house.'

He nodded; it was almost as if he wanted to be entrusted to the police. She found the gear and they slid forwards into darkness.

20

Once they had broken into the house – Ruth had realised with horror that she hadn't got the keys and they'd had to force an entry by the terrace – her immediate instinct was to leave. In driving Eduardo away from Calanda she'd done more than her duty by him; now her plan was to find José's parents – perhaps even José would be there, and the local *guardias* would come and arrest Eduardo here. But something made her hover on the point of her departure, as if reluctant to turn her back so quickly on this moment in her life.

They were dripping together on a rug scattered with broken glass, Eduardo still holding the loose railing from the balustrade which he'd used to break the shutters and the window. Would he try to stop her from going? Ruth didn't think so – she felt as if an unspoken bargain had been established between them since their talk in the car; having escaped from the old man's nephew, perhaps Eduardo would even be relieved to be in the hands of the police?

She searched for the book of matches in her pocket but it was gone – she couldn't remember where she'd lost it. There was a spark, and the flame of a cigarette lighter poured from his hand.

'No lights,' he growled.

'It's the storm. There's a candle.'

Her hand moved an iron holder on the front of the piano. The flame brushed close to the wick.

'Here.'

She took it from him and bent it closer: a sepia light grew over the pages of music. By it she saw his unshaven cheeks, his brown dog-eyes, his moustache lank from the rain. She felt a momentary warmth for him and a regret that he'd travelled too far: there could be no saving him from himself.

Reason told her to leave. She was tempted, momentarily, to kiss him goodbye; the thought of the texture of another cheek stopped her in her tracks. Then she was making for the door; as she'd anticipated he didn't try to stop her going out on to the landing, or feeling her way down into the hall.

She froze at the bottom of the stairs. Outside was the throb of an engine. Could it be José? She turned the latch and opened the heavy door a few inches: rain tickled her face. Stationary, further down the street, blazed a pair of double headlamps. The engine expired as the lights died. She'd already closed the door and was racing upstairs when she heard the door of the jeep click shut and the murmur of voices.

Mierda, she thought. One moment's hesitation – her damned sentiment – and she'd given his pursuers time. Suddenly she realised her stupidity: they must have seen the car outside. But how had they known where to come?

As she burst into the living-room the long window slammed, wiping out the candle flame. There was no sound from Eduardo. Opening the window, a shard of glass fell on her hand, slicing her wrist; then she was out on the terrace, rain full in her face. The bare branches of the fig tree creaked and scuffled; suddenly she saw the beam of a torch ploughing through the rain – one of the men was coming round the back. At the same moment the iron knocker on the front door crashed inside the house, and Ruth knew she was trapped.

She scuttled through the house, desperate for a way out. The walls seemed to give way before her, one room unfolding into the next; in a lightning flash the shadow of some shutters flapped like the wings of a great bird. Opening that window she let in a bombardment of thunder – it was too dark to judge the distance to the street below. A small back staircase wound down to the servants' quarters, but as she felt her way down she remembered that each window on the ground floor was barred. Entering the kitchen she heard the scour of Eduardo's breath. She controlled herself.

'Eduardo – they're here. The lighter!'

'You've got it.'

The scratch of the wheel on her finger tip, and the blue flame revealed him through the door into the pantry, squatting down to struggle with something on the floor.

'No!' she said. 'You'll be shut in!'

'There's a way out of the cellar.' He seemed quite sober now. 'Don't know if it's still there.' He had got his hands around the wooden hatch and was heaving it up; then he was sinking into the black.

'Wait,' she said.

At first, when she dashed forwards, it was just to give him the light: she had an idea that if she could prove she was English the men might leave her alone, even though she'd been with him in the church. But just as she reached the hatch there was another blow on the front door, and the darkness seemed to beckon – besides, perhaps there was a way of escape?

'Close it,' Eduardo croaked up to her as she began to descend, so she had to balance on the iron ladder and lower the door down on top of them. She missed a rung and landed with a thud on the earth floor.

'This way!' he murmured, and had already gone; she had to scrabble for the lighter on the sandy earth; then she twisted it on. The flame caused a witches' sabbath of shadows as she passed through one room, then another, weaving through the dancing forms of great pots, suspended hams and farm instruments. She found Eduardo in the deepest part of the cellar single-handedly trying to move an old pedal loom from among a forest of broken chairs, leaning oil paintings, calfskin books . . .

'I think it's behind there,' he said, indicating an oak sideboard against the wall. 'For God's sake, help.'

Their grunts and whispers were frightful in the darkness while, by the intermittent glow of the lighter flame, they worked to clear away the things in front. Between cursing her foolishness for having let herself get involved, and her terror of hearing the creak of the hatch, Ruth racked her brains to remember what José had told her about the tunnel. Had he been up it? Was it still passable? They were just shifting the leather trunk when she had a sudden strong impression that something was wrong. That was it – pausing to relight the flame, she saw that the lid had been cleared. Opening it at once, she delved among rags and straw. The cool caress of leather; a lightness – the holster was empty.

She relit the flame. 'Your father's gun,' she said. 'Did you take it?'

Eduardo caught his breath. His face registered astonishment as he stared from her to the open chest and back again; then he took a dark object out of his anorak. Even by the lighter flame she could see it was a different weapon, more compact-looking – and new.

A floorboard groaned. They froze, but no more noise came. Eduardo pocketed the gun, and signed her to hold the light aloft; then he strained at the sideboard, finally budging it a few inches: something shattered inside. The flame licked into a gash in the bricks.

'You first,' he said.

They climbed into the narrow cavity behind the wall. Ruth's foot jammed between sharp rocks, but she wrenched it out and moved on, making room for Eduardo to wedge himself in: she could smell him at her back in the confined space. Edging gingerly forwards, she came to a high ledge and got a foothold.

'Eduardo – come,' she whispered.

Ahead of her was a roughly hewn flight of steps. She took the first up, then the second, then five or six, bending her head beneath a ceiling which lowered sharply. She found she'd come to another crevice like the one below but, pressing on the lighter, she saw that there was more tunnel beyond. The flame was scorching her thumb. She went on without it, raising her arms to protect her head. In the enclosed darkness, she had the odd sensation that the place was familiar, perhaps from her dreams. She struggled on, grazing her hand. The passage was still rising, but more gently now and finally, turning a corner, the walls were gone and she was stumbling over a bed of rubble and broken rocks.

It was dark in this stomach of the hill and the silence was dense, the slightest sound magnified by the walls. She sparked the lighter and saw the phrase 'Martínez – 1837' incised in the rock among other names and dates. Exhausted from the effort of climbing, she sat as best she could on a heap of rubble and gazed into the flame while Eduardo leaned against the wall, his finger tracing one of the names. She wondered how long it would be until the fuel in the tiny cylinder ran out.

Suddenly the anorak squeaked, and Eduardo pulled out a crushed packet of cigarettes and tapped the last one out on to his palm. Before she could stop him he had broken it in two and was offering her a piece.

'I don't smoke.'

'Not an English habit?'

She did not reply; yet something made her put the half-cigarette into her pocket.

He bent down to light his portion at the flame.

'Listen!' she hissed; but there was no sound from the tunnel behind. The stub's tip glowed where Eduardo was standing by the wall.

She whispered, 'How did you know about this place?'

'My father showed me it when I was a child.' He took a deep drag. 'Something nasty happened here in the war.'

Of course, she thought. 'What was that?'

'It was when the anarchists came, I think. Something about a village curate holing up here – folk from the village brought him food. Then someone split on him. They walled the place up and forgot about the bloke.'

'And you're sure it's open now?'

'It used to be.'

He tossed the butt away. 'Come on, English girl.'

Her legs ached as she made her way through a small stone-built archway into a room whose floor was a metre down and piled with rubble. She hesitated, so this time it was Eduardo who went ahead while she held the lighter up to the ceiling. It was terrifying following him over those broken rocks in darkness knowing that ahead was a wall; then she felt the warmth of a broad hand feeling blindly around her head, and grabbed it, thankful to be helped up on to the ledge on which he was standing.

The flame flickered again on the walls. They were of a darker stone, now, a long uninterrupted fold of rock along one side, the other chipped and broken. There was a humid chill in the air, penetrating their clothes and making the tongue of gas shiver – the odour of soil after rain. Eduardo preceded her again, taking the light this time as the tunnel sloped alarmingly downwards before meeting another cleft and more roughly formed steps. These were so steep as to be exhausting; she got the impression, as she dragged herself up, rested for a moment, dragged herself up again, that she was following him almost vertically up a narrow crevice. Sometimes the steps had crumbled and they had to make do with natural footholds in the rock. Then, with an alarming abruptness, they were no longer climbing: the ground on which they were standing seemed to be an armature of sloping hulks separated by crevices, like the floor of a mouth.

Ruth stood for a while to get her breath back, wondering why Eduardo didn't relight the flame. Her first sensation was of a cold freshness penetrating the coat of dust covering her face and hands and which dried her mouth as she licked her lips. There was a sound of rain falling on earth. Already she was aware of the faintest glimmer of light, an irregular panel, like a window of darkly stained glass behind the statues of a baroque altarpiece. But as her eyes dwelt on this, absorbing with relief the fact that the dim light was the sky just before dawn, one of the statues moved, causing a small cascade of stones. She held her breath.

Eduardo was still, too, presumably because he had also seen the figure in the cave mouth, barely visible against the sky. She remembered the men behind – but there was no sound from the tunnel.

'The light,' she murmured.

'Ruth,' a voice said from somewhere. 'You too?'

The words answered themselves from the walls. The voice sounded familiar. Then the blue flame hissed and she saw José – or a version of him, for there was something utterly remote about the pale, rigid-faced man standing slightly above them on the rocky floor. From the look of his drawn cheeks and shaded eyes she would have said he was exhausted if she didn't have the impression that he was so angry he was himself afraid. He had one hand in his coat pocket.

'Pepe – I'm glad you're here,' Eduardo said hoarsely: the pet name sounded like a last resort. Turning slightly, she could make out the shape of his anorak where he half-crouched beside a bulwark of rock.

She could hear the tautness in her voice as she spoke. 'José – those men are in the house – they could be coming up –'

'Walk past me,' he said. 'And leave.'

The last word came back.

'I only wanted –'

His next exclamation was made inaudible by the cave's resonance, but its meaning was clear. She bit her lip, determined at least not to move.

Apparently resigned to this he went on, 'We've been talking to someone, Eduardo. Listen . . .'

A rustling sound. For a moment, seeing a movement of his coat, Ruth feared José was going to take out a gun; but the next thing she was aware of was a sudden blare of noise inside the cave. Suddenly this resolved itself into the quavery sound of a voice resounding in the rocks; it was as though the cave itself had come alive. Her heart was in her mouth until she realised that the sudden drop in volume had come from José adjusting the control of the pocket tape-recorder he had taken from his coat and was holding in his hand. A good part of the tape had already gone before she was able to work out that the voice whose ghost answered from the walls was that of Eduardo's mother, Emilia:

> . . . Don't ask me why he could never put it behind him. I believe, now, that that's why there was all that trouble before . . . And now this . . . Everyone knew what the police were like in those days. If only his father had been alive, he'd have had someone to turn to . . .
> José: Did he ever talk about my brother, Emilia?
> Emilia: You know the truth, or you wouldn't be asking me.

A higher voice on the tape – Ruth recognised Elena:

> It was because of him, then, that he died?
> Emilia: No, no. It wasn't simple. I really don't know what happened. It's wrong of you to torment me . . .
> José: Please, Aunt. Just a minute more.

The old lady sighed before going on:

> It was the poor man who's dead who told me, may he rest in peace. On one of those occasions when my son turned up in his house he kept asking if he knew what had happened to Juan. So you see, the poor man himself told me, when he was worried about Eduardo, that it had been Eduardo who turned him in, and he did die at the hands of the police. But he thought it would be better – poor man – if my son didn't know . . .

The gas in the lighter had run out, but there was enough natural light now for her to distinguish the shaking of Eduardo's body where he sat, his face in his hands. José switched off the machine.

There was a rockfall behind them; then a murmur from the tunnel – Eduardo looked up.

'You're not leaving.' José said.

169

'For God's sake, José – let him go.'

'No.'

It was then that José took out the gun. Even without seeing it properly Ruth knew it was the one from the cellar, and her horror was increased by the memory of its weight and the texture of the webbing on the butt.

'Out of here. Ruth. I told you – out!'

There was a louder movement in the tunnel behind.

'It's them!' she cried.

Then Eduardo's hand moved to his pocket and he lurched towards the daylight, gun in hand, accompanied by an echo of falling stones.

In the next few moments each of them acted at that basic level of impulse which makes the actions of animals – even the frenzy of hunter and hunted – elide into a single motion. Everything happened so fast that it seemed to take no more than the time between Eduardo's scramble and the last waves of echo this set off. And if one rhythm ran through all of them, its ebb and flow was matched by the cave's acoustic which blended their movements into a developing cacophony.

Eduardo had dashed forwards so quickly that the first she saw of him was reaching the daylight, not looking back, the anorak billowing behind him. But this sight only lasted an instant, for it was José who seized her attention now, as he released the catch on his gun before raising his arm to fire.

She would never know how she found the energy to leap across the cave floor and grab his arm. The weight of her landing caught him off balance and both of them crashed awkwardly on to the rock, slithering on to a bed of stones. At the same moment a shot rang out, its sound ricocheting about the walls.

Had Eduardo got away? She couldn't tell, and just as José was wresting himself free from her she was dazzled by a torch and heard an urgent murmur of voices. She tried to see behind the light, but a shower of grit and pebbles dislodged by José standing just above her filled her eyes. There was a whiff of smoke. Remaining low – she expected to be deafened by another shot at any moment, though she could feel the warmth of the gun that had gone off by her hand, she was puzzled to hear a woman shouting and a thunderous tramp of boots. Then the torch had gone, and through a film of dust and shale she saw the face of a civil guard – the black winged hat was unmistakable as he turned back in the cave mouth, hand-gun at the ready – waiting for his colleague to jump down and vanish with him down the side of the hill.

At last she felt a hand on her arm and, opening her eyes once again, saw the gold hair and pale face of Elena by the faint light of dawn.

She was still confused as, grazed and bleeding, she staggered out on the Spanish woman's arm to feel the drizzle on her face. And it was only then, by extracting the memory of certain actions from the pandemonium which had surged and receded in the cave, that she began to understand that it was Elena, accompanied by two civil guards, who had emerged from the tunnel to find Eduardo on the run and José gesturing to them to follow. Eduardo's pursuers were nowhere to be seen.

It was not relief she felt but a kind of absence from herself as, blood throbbing in her head, she sank down on a boulder just outside the cave. Elena was saying something, proffering a handkerchief; but all Ruth was really conscious of was the grey reality of light on stone. And it took some time before her vision spread to include José, standing a few paces away with his back to them as he looked out over the cliff's edge, and the single wall of the ruined castle against the sky.

Then she heard the grind of an engine at its limit and, just below the hillside, saw the pale flash of Eduardo's car cross the road between two outcrops of rock. Another vehicle followed, but this time it was not the jeep but a van with the red sign-light of the civil guard.

171

21

Ruth winced, causing the guard's daughter to murmur, 'It's bound to hurt.'

She was sitting with her back against the rail of an old-fashioned stove as the glossy-haired girl dabbed antiseptic on to the cut on her wrist. Beyond her bowed head and through a barred window she could just make out part of the jeep outside; Elena and José were still talking to the guard in the next room.

She had the impression, as she would again later that day, that her feelings were not behaving as they should. She ought to have experienced immense relief at the knowledge that Eduardo's pursuers were at last behind bars – they were in another part of the building waiting to be taken to the prison in Zaragoza. They had still been searching the old house when Elena and the two guards had arrived the night before. Ruth's extreme tiredness, and the pain of her bruises, did not prevent her from realising that what had happened in the cave could have been much worse. Why then was she conscious of the sense of something unresolved?

The murmur of voices from the next room gave her the answer. The change in José had been terrifying; not least because it was the development of an aspect of him she had known without understanding. The unexpected silence in response to a question of hers, the solitary walks – all that made sense now. If sense was the word, for what she'd seen in José was the readiness to kill. The thought of the two imprisoned men raised the question: shouldn't he have been arrested, too? She was sure that, as they came out of the tunnel, the guards' torch must have licked the gun lying on the cave floor. Elena had certainly seen it. Yet from the sound of the next-door voices it seemed as if they were talking amiably.

Later José told her that the news had come by telephone. The first sign of it was the urgency of their voices as they emerged on to the steps so that, afraid of missing something, she stopped the guard's daughter and went to the window to shout, 'Wait!' Elena was already by her car. Ruth barely had time to thank the girl and roll up her sleeve before she was out in the street, expecting as before to be stuck on the back seat, leaning forwards to try to piece together the information which filtered back to her. But this time José got in first and she was in the front as they set off along the Calanda road.

By the time they arrived she had gathered what the news was, and anything she had not understood was made clear by the sight which met them as they turned a bend and came to a halt on the verge. Of the brief and savage accident which had taken place there remained only the parked civil guard van which, she later knew, had met Eduardo's speeding car head on in the dawn light; the police vehicle which had been giving chase; a gaping tear in the arrowed crash barrier into which Eduardo had been forced to swerve before his car had plunged into the reservoir below.

Getting out, she smelled the freshness of the country after rain: damp earth, the tang of manure, a fragrance of woodsmoke. They were at a point where the River Guadalope, making its swift way down from the massive weight of the higher reservoir, broadened into the stretch of water which she had driven past with Eduardo the night before. A chill breeze made the broom and rosemary clumps shiver by the side of the road.

In the next hour or so it seemed to her that time slowed down, distending the pattern of events into a dimension measured only by the gradual increase of light. The noises she heard – the guards' voices, the gearing-up of cars and slamming doors, the clap of wavelets against the shore – seemed detached from their sources. And perhaps it was her own exhaustion, but the actions of the police, the lengthy preparations to retrieve the submerged car, seemed almost furtive, a clandestine operation performed under the cover of mist.

Some time before, Elena had come across to where she was seated on a concrete wall to say she was going to drive on to Calanda – did she want to come? – and it was only once she'd driven off, leaving José and her with the guards, that Ruth realised she must have gone to tell Teresa what had happened. The memory of the conversation she'd had with her had become a bright fragment among the images of the night, which seemed like a dream of the sort it's a relief to let the morning erase.

It was daylight by the time a pick-up truck arrived. The water was so high that it was difficult to position it so that it could be driven forwards with the car; finally another part of the crash barrier was removed and it was stationed on a stretch of mud just below. Later still a couple of men in wet-suits dived down to try to fix ropes to the car, though they were hampered by the lack of oxygen masks. Finally the ropes tautened, and the truck's wheels began to churn the mud.

Ruth didn't know why, but the ratcheting truck, the interest of people on the road, didn't seem to impinge on her – though this feeling didn't detract from the importance of what was happening. It relieved her to be able to walk past an ambulance with its back doors open parked by the side of the road to a place where an outcrop of rock extended above the water, concealing the commotion on the shore. Staring down she let her mind wander, seeing, as the images were swept into her vision by the stream, the minarets of the Church of the Pilar shivering in the brown tide of the Ebro; three children, one much older than the others, standing by the side of the reservoir; the shadows of an underwater street; a blue T-shirt floating just below the water's surface in the dazzling sun . . .

Opposite, on the far bank, the bare branches of a cluster of poplars stuck up like roots, as if the trees were growing downwards into the earth. High up on each bank the shoulders of a broken bridge, one of those semi-circular structures reminiscent of bandits and mule trains, seemed like the reflection of a complete bridge shattered by the sun's wake. The sun lay like a new peseta in a sea of mud.

She was so absorbed in contemplation of this upside-down world that she missed the agony of the five or six failed attempts to drag up the car, and its eventual lurch back up on to the road. Later José would tell her he'd been foolish enough to expect to see Eduardo still upright in the driver's seat as it came up, and that it had shocked him for a moment that the car had looked empty. She missed all this, and by the time she returned to the scene there was only mud streaming off the car where it lay beached on the shore, and a grey blanket laid over what she knew to be the matter of Eduardo.

It must have been her tiredness which at first prevented her from recognising Pedro and the cake-shop girl sitting opposite her on the far side of the room. Both of them were smoking. From time to time, Pedro would pass an ash-tray to the girl who, having flicked ash into it, would hand it back to him, and he would replace it on a chair beside him.

Neither of them is thinking, she thought, and nor am I, as the ash-tray was set down for the fourth time on the empty chair.

She and José had followed the ambulance in a police van to the headquarters in Calanda, and she was sitting in a waiting-room while Eduardo's mother and Teresa, accompanied by the others, were identifying the drowned man. She could hear the drums still buzzing like a hive of bees in another section of the town. The drummers would have gathered again in the wide square, among them a few, exhausted but proud, who had managed to keep going all night.

With a start she realised that the door had opened and a group of people were coming out, causing Pedro and his girlfriend to rise to their feet. Teresa's mother had appeared first, supported by her blotchy-faced daughter. Then came her father, José's parents, and finally, wheeled by José, a stately old lady in a wheelchair who she realised must be Eduardo's mother.

The room was suddenly full of a barely subdued chatter of

Spanish. As the old lady was addressing a guard, her silver-headed walking stick slithered on to the floor. Stepping forwards to restore it to her, Ruth caught sight of the tiny steel yoke and arrows, badge of the Falange, on the lapel of her coat.

The powdered face loosened into a courteous smile and the old lady's voice crackled, 'Thank you, my daughter.'

'*De nada.*'

As the others were starting to leave, Ruth said to Elena, 'Is he in there?'

'Go on,' a guard said.

Only his face was not covered by the blanket; its colour was like that of the bottled reptiles in her school laboratory. She could not tell if it was this idea or some elemental instinct for preservation which cut her off from the distant tremor of the drums and the murmur of last-minute arrangements in the next room. She had wanted to see him; yet she found herself looking away to a polythene bag near the table in which lay a wrist-watch, a ballpoint pen, a leather-bound diary. There was no sign of the gun.

She forced herself to look again. At the texture of pores – so large he could have died from goose-pimples. At the bulk of the eyes behind closed lids. At the moustache and grey carved mouth. As she looked she became aware that she was touching something in her pocket; she brought it out, and the half cigarette lay on her palm in a litter of tobacco.

'Are you all right?' Elena asked.

But before she could answer there was a change in the room; a dislocation of air which at first made her think a light had been switched off or a window closed. Someone's head turned. And then Ruth understood that a continuum of noise so deep, so invariable that she had forgotten its existence had ceased at a single stroke. She thought – as she realised the drums had stopped – that it was like discovering that a person you loved was no longer there.

Somewhere a church clock was striking. The others' voices were mute. And in the intense, the almost visible, silence she could hear the sound of her own breathing.

She staggered and reached out to hold Elena, as if it were the floor, not her legs, which had folded under her.

SPANISH DRUMS

PART FOUR

EASTER DAY

22

On the road from Teruel to Alcañiz the bus follows the tracks of a
railway on the right. Sometimes close to the road, swinging into perspective like an object in a dream, sometimes on the far side of a field
of stubble, alone and with only the crows for company, a station will
appear: tall, Alphonsine, utilitarian, its roof a cage of beams across
the sky. Now only the hills are visible through the torn-out windows,
the partitions which used to divide the passengers' entrance from the
ticket-office and the ticket-office from the station-master's room
fallen into rubble; the track itself runs like a fault-line through the
bare fields, providing a lean pasture for the flocks which are herded
along it in the evenings, discarding a frail cacophony of bells.

One such station is that of Alcañiz, one of the larger places on the
derelict line. To its south there has not been a railway since the war,
but Alcañiz station continued to serve as a terminus for the northern
section of the line until the seventies: it still has its tiled roof and a
metal canopy shading the single platform.

To reach the station, walk down the Calle Mayor past the disused
cinema to the corner of the bridge where a bar clings on over the river
bed next to the modern statue of the Virgin with a concrete canopy.
Cross the bridge and, instead of joining the main road to Zaragoza,
take the second turning on the right. After a long line of buildings,
one of which is a former flour factory – you can just make out the
faded blue letters on the wall – you will come to a cobbled stretch of
road bordered by two rows of plane trees. When the sun goes down in

dust behind the hills its beams fall diagonally through the leaves, scattering shade across the road. This soon stops, however: the avenue breaks off on the left, then on the right, and the road curves round to lead over an irrigation ditch into the station forecourt.

The station is a symmetrical building, consisting of a long ground floor with three groups of triple-arched door-windows and a smaller rectangle with three more windows on top. The windows are shuttered and boarded up. To the right a number of acacia trees divide the ditch from two or three sheds or loading bays. The gates are open: the sheds are used as barns for tractors and storing hay. Turning left and crossing the floor of the sheds will bring you out to face the line on the other side.

There must be fifteen or twenty tracks tangled like grooves in a skating rink, some radiating from a concrete carousel. Beyond the junction is a brief no-man's land, then a grove of olive trees which extends until the hill becomes steep and rocky. On the side of the hill stands the sanctuary of the Virgin of Pueyos, curtained by cypresses. To the right the line is bridged by the road to the sanctuary, to the left it runs past the main railway shed, its girders black against the sky. All is broken, rusted or bent out of shape; the shoots of a virulent weed stick up, dagger-like between the sleepers, making a vertical junction with the sky; an old lever for changing the points gives only slightly if you pull it towards you, its mechanism choked. Under the canopy the sign 'Alcañiz' hangs from a metal bracket.

A faded blue butterfly fluttered against a wall. Ruth followed its flight out of light into darkness, then into sun again as it alighted on a fennel stalk in the dewy grass. Although it was early the church bells could be heard calling people to Mass: their distant clamour carried on the chill air. She was leaning on the bonnet of José's van in the station forecourt, letting the sun warm her face.

It was José who had suggested a drive. She'd been sitting at the breakfast table, alone with the small array of Easter cards from relations and friends – messages from another world, enjoying the feeling of having slept for over eight hours. The short rest she'd managed to snatch the day before, interrupted by Elena coming to say that the police wanted to speak to her, had not been enough to prevent her stumbling and repeating herself during the interview, protracting it far more than was necessary. On her return José had driven to his parents', so they had not properly spoken to each other during Easter Saturday, and her general sense of relief was tempered by a recurrence of unease about him. The policeman who'd interviewed her hadn't mentioned his action in the cave and she hadn't raised it either, though it seemed like a flaw in a glass.

It was with mixed feelings, therefore, that she'd agreed to the drive. She hadn't known – or asked – where they were going; the derelict station was a place where they had once or twice come to talk until she'd told him it depressed her. When they arrived he'd said, 'I just want to be on my own for a few minutes – I won't be long,' leaving her on the forecourt by the van. According to her wrist-watch he'd been five – no, ten minutes already.

She stretched her hand through the window and sounded the horn. For a moment there was a drop in the chorus of birds in the trees around. A pair of magpies flashed over by the road; a lizard scuttled into a crack. Already the ground was drying: in a few weeks the earth under the olives would be dry as bread.

The bird-song tentatively resumed. She hooted again, then began to walk towards the hay-barns and the sunlight beyond.

She heard them first of all on the breeze, the sharp yelp of the dog bouncing alongside, the harsh cry of the shepherd as he skimmed a stone, their faint bleating through the tuneless bells. They were a flock of grubby sheep, straggly fur dangling from their sides, among them a few glossy goats whose elastic mouths extended to envelop stalks of fennel and cow parsley.

Standing in the doorway of the station building she saw smashed glass, torn scraps of posters on the floor with cartoons of a satisfied traveller and the slogan: 'Papá – come by train'. She called, but there was no reply; yet stepping out again on to the platform she could not see José among the weeds or the olive trees beyond. The stairs

183

creaked as she went up.

He was standing at one of the upstairs windows, looking out through a jagged hole in the glass at the town amassed on its two hills; the sky dazzled beyond his head. He must have heard the squeak of a floorboard as she came in, for he turned and leaned back with his bottom against the sill, the wind ruffling his hair.

Neither spoke for a while. Finally she said, 'You really hurt me, you know, pushing me like that – I'm bruised all over.'

'I'm sorry.' He took her hand, but she withdrew it, disliking herself not for needing, but for obtaining an apology.

'You did well to stop me the other night. I – I don't know what came over me, I was so –'

No word came.

'You were right to feel like that, I suppose, but . . .' She hesitated. 'Did you really want to kill him?'

He gave a swift nod, concealing the effort of the admission.

'I just can't tell you how angry I was. You know I just worshipped my brother when I was a child – he was older and seemed to know everything, I suppose – and that Eduardo had done that and not told me about it, though I'd done so much to help him . . .'

'He wanted to tell you.'

'Perhaps . . . Anyway, I found myself asking, what would Juan have done if it had been me? Then I had to find the gun. You'd reminded me of it.'

She nodded.

'Nothing would stop me until I'd got it in my hand. I didn't think – yes, I'll find him and kill him, but I wanted to confront him and get him to admit he'd screwed us all . . .' A deep furrow creased his narrow brow; the skin was damp with sweat.

'But how did you mean to find him?'

'I only knew he was in Calanda. Earlier Teresa had phoned my parents' house to say she'd spoken to you and that you'd seen him at the drums. I half-hoped I wouldn't find him, but there was a chance . . .'

'But you were in the cave.'

'Wait. I found the gun in the chest. At first I thought I wouldn't be able to load it, and then suddenly it was done – it was as if my hands knew how to do it. The next thing was to get to Calanda. I hadn't got the van because I'd left it at my sister's and we'd come in her car, so I went back and begged her to lend me it. She'd managed to get our aunt to bed. I think she could sense how I was feeling because she tried to dissuade me, saying there was a storm. Then the lights went out. I knew I had to get to Calanda, so I told Elena I needed to talk to her – Calanda was the only place where we'd get something to eat; we had to get out of my parents' house. Finally she agreed – against her will, especially as just as we were going out the sky really opened. It was she who saw his car. We'd driven past it, parked by the roadside, Zaragoza plates and everything. It was obvious he was in the old house. I could feel the weight of the gun inside my coat . . .'

'So Elena went to the police?'

'Yes. The local guard is a friend of the family. He woke his colleague, Elena began to explain . . . My mind was on just one thing: find Eduardo. So I said, "I'll be back now," and went out. It was raining torrents. I went straight to the old house. Then I saw the jeep –'

She interrupted. 'What made those men come to Belmonte?'

'Didn't they follow you?'

'I didn't see them.'

He shrugged. 'Perhaps they were following Eduardo the first day, when he found me at the house. Anyway, the police arrived. Instead of waiting, I started up the hill. I thought there was a chance he'd have thought of the tunnel and, if not, the men would have got him.'

'So when I warned you about them in the cave you knew they'd been arrested?'

'It seemed likely, unless something had gone wrong. You know the rest,' he added.

Telling the story had drained his face of colour. Ruth felt she could understand now how desperate he'd felt – yet understanding wasn't enough.

'Stopping me was the best thing you've done,' he said. 'I won't for-get it.'

She avoided his look.

'I just wonder if . . . Perhaps if I hadn't lost my temper like that . . .'

He had turned and was staring out again at the drifting town. She stepped back and, perching on another window-sill, gazed down through a hole in the shutters at a patch of entangled, rusted rails.

The sight of them put her in mind of her trip south and the many journeys she had made over the peninsula. She thought of the holi-days she'd had with her parents as a child, of the station in Castile where the father of a family she was staying with had been kind enough to have a train stopped for her so that she wouldn't have to wait. She thought of the night expresses clanking and flashing beneath her balcony in Madrid, and the storm through which her train had slithered up into Granada. Did her journey end here? In this overgrown tangle of weeds and memories?

She had been so absorbed in her thoughts that she had not seen José leave the room. She put up the collar of her jacket less against the cold than against a gust of loneliness. I must go, she thought, realising at that instant that she did not only mean the deserted station but Teruel. Glancing back at the empty room she thought how the troubles of Eduardo had distracted her from her own care-less treatment of José.

He was leaning against the van. Neither spoke as he drove them across the river and up into the town. A few weeks before she might have tried to make her feelings more acceptable by sharing them with him, but she knew now that there were decisions which had to be made alone, and that she owed it to herself as well as to him to make them. She wished that she had known this before, for she feared that it might be too late now not to lose a friend.

The sight of the modern anarchists' red circled 'A' sprayed on a wall reminded her of her official reason for being in Teruel. She didn't feel that she had yet found the key to unifying her material, yet she sensed that the idea was closer than it had been. She had anyway known for some time that she had reached the point at which her interviews were confirming previous ones rather than revealing much that was new. The truth was that soon – by this summer, perhaps – she would have done enough to be able to complete her work in England, whether she liked it or not. It was ironic how this conviction coincided with the impression that she had gone beyond her thesis. She felt she stood a better chance of writing it now that it seemed so much less important to her.

Suddenly the van was surrounded by a gaggle of pedestrians – ladies in best coats, little girls in tartan skirts and boys in bright bomber jackets; their menfolk, with pressed trousers and freshly combed hair, would be snatching cups of coffee in busy bars.

'It's the procession,' José said. 'We'd better go round the other way.'

Ruth was seized by the same excitement she'd felt before the drums. 'Don't you want to see?'

His look fell on her like a shadow; then his face broke into a smile. He shook his head quickly. As she kissed him on the cheek, there was a rhythmic thump on the roof of the car from the fists of some passing schoolboys. José frowned; a car blew its horn behind; then Ruth was walking up the street into the square alone.

She had to push her way through a crowd to get to the town hall. At the top of a flight of stairs she passed into a high room where the town's dignitaries, councillors and civil servants and their families, were chatting, glasses of wine in hand. She slipped out on to the balcony behind a group of well-dressed children scrambling for a place at the draped balustrade.

The square below looked like a stage-set: people strolling in a shaft of light. Under the arcade of the Bar Central a group of older men in berets talked and leaned on their sticks. A traffic policeman was directing cars away from the square.

A small uniformed band struck up a *pasodoble* up on the steps of the church; their incompetence made her smile. A pair of lackeys came out of the main door in red eighteenth-century livery, and the town-crier with a trumpet. These were followed by that day's float – a large wooden Easter egg covered in crimson velvet topped with a tasselled rope stretching down to the official who walked beside it. Four men swung it along, two at each end. Behind this straggled a bunch of children in regional costume: boys in red sashes and black waistcoats and girls in pleated dresses with flowered shawls. They made their way down the ramp into the square.

The band switched to a tragic march. Then came a trio of choirboys, one swaying a censer, choking smoke puffed up on the breeze. The handsome young curate who had helped Eduardo preceded the parish priest, who was bearing the Sacrament in its gilded pyx beneath a canopy held by four acolytes. It was like a scene from a genre painting of the twenties, Ruth thought, or a procession on one of the old pre-war newsreels she had seen in the Madrid Filmoteca; in those days people prostrated themselves before the Host instead of just crossing themselves as they were doing now. Behind the canopy strolled the mayor and two colleagues in red sashes, then a huddle of men in suits, chatting casually as though the procession were an unavoidable chore.

Now the parade had curved round in a circle until the float was in front of the bar. They all stopped; the priest took the end of the rope connected to the egg, and when he tugged a second time – at first nothing happened – it fell open in segments and five terrified doves fluttered about before swooping up to the gables above the library. Music crackled on a public address system and a distorted voice announced that the Lord had risen, and asked them to recite the Lord's Prayer. Ruth shut her eyes and whispered the words, but couldn't finish – the thought of the egg made her giggle; it was so different from the opulent Palm Sunday of the south.

The band played the *Himno Nacional* and the bells of the church rang as the whole procession returned up the ramp.

'I haven't been thinking about him,' Elena said suddenly.

Ruth turned to find José's sister standing next to her as the children, bored now, plunged back into the room. 'I've spent at least twenty minutes not thinking about Eduardo, just watching that ridiculous piece of hocus pocus. I need to sit down . . .' She returned into the room where space was made for her on a red armchair in which she sat while some of the teachers from the school gathered around her.

Down in the square people were passing or standing to converse in a faltering sun. Ruth walked up the ramp and looked out over the roof of the closed market and the blocks of flats beyond. At the end of a street the hills were like spent sand at the foot of an hour-glass. In a few months they would be crumbling rock, held in place by a tangle of flat thistles and leggy gorse. Through the doors of the church behind her filtered a chant and the scrape of chairs.

She stepped into the dark hubbub, wondering how its builders could have justified putting up a church which, with its expanse of glossy floor and neo-classical arches, would never be full: had the town not expanded as they hoped? A baby wailed; the congregation rose; everywhere was the squeak and shuffle of shoes. Behind her a wooden door squealed and hissed, distributing brightness. The hotel proprietress, in a navy coat, bent a knee and crossed herself before leaving. A father bounced his son on his arm, and the child gazed at her, jet-eyed, its thumb in its mouth.

The people sat – wheat in a wind – and the curate stood in white at the lectern.

'He is risen,' he said. 'He is not here. Behold the place where they laid Him . . .' He began to speak about the power of Redemption, of hope, of the meaning of suffering. Death was in life, he said. It gave our lives meaning, for it was the prospect of death that made us think about the shape of our lives, about the effects we had on others. The lesson of death was that we only had one life. To make a mess of it – or not to work to put the mess right – was to give death too much ground.

'Christ was right,' he went on, 'to think of death not as a master but as a servant. The Resurrection shows us there is something beyond death, something much more powerful, and perhaps our attainment of that depends on our having the courage to see how death can be useful to us . . .'

Wandering up the steep slope above the town Ruth reflected that it was his work to put the mess right that had once made her envy José; the methodical, quiet work bringing about the changes his country deserved. Now she felt that she, too, though in a state barely distinguishable from panic, had achieved something comparable. In preventing him from shooting his cousin she had saved him – and given Eduardo a chance.

She wondered about Eduardo's last moments. Driving along that road, he must have known he was no longer being pursued by the old man's nephew but by the *guardia civil*. Perhaps it might have crossed his mind to slow down and accept the inevitability of imprisonment. Yet how could Eduardo, of all people, have trusted the police? It occurred to her that in the split second in which he'd seen the second van hurtling round the bend in front of him he was at last confronting himself, the self which was not clear to him – had not been clear since the decision, years before in Madrid, to split himself in two.

One life, the curate had said. But knowing how to shape it was so hard, and you had to accept that there would be mistakes, wrong turnings, long periods of infertility. It was no good ignoring them; you had to look back and feel your face burn. Wasn't that the point of history? There were many ways of confronting the past. Talking to someone. A notebook. A tape-recorder . . .

Eduardo had been incapable of this. It seemed to her now that, among other things, his murder of the old man had been an attempt to kill history. It was what the anarchists had tried to do – and the dictatorship; and in the end both had failed.

Up on the flat summit of the town there was a row of cars parked in front of the castle and a hotel employee was helping a tourist to pack the boot of his car; the rest of the family were taking snapshots of each other by the parapet.

Clambering up behind the castle, she looked out over the plain to the narrow chimney of the power station on the horizon, the sierra over to the east. The sun landed on her face and, high up beneath a faint ripple of clouds, a sparrowhawk floated on the air. The river below flashed; the trees were a haze of green; almond blossom had started to come out in the orchards on the far side. At that distance it looked white, but she knew that from close up it would have a slight violet tinge, the colour of a fingernail.

Below her was the place where she'd buried the goldfinch months before. She imagined, beneath the earth, the tiny cage of ivory bones – if the crows hadn't dispersed them. The wind bore the dryness of the hills. She noticed she was crying; yet she was smiling, too, and she knew it would always be like this: crying and smiling were two sides of the same coin.

Her hand delved into her pocket and rested it on her palm. There were no markings on it at all, stating its origin or how much it was worth – perhaps this was anarchist policy, or perhaps in the war there had been no time for such things. She tilted it a little, darkening it briefly; then flung it out over the cliff's edge. It was too light to travel far.

She walked down into the town's din: the barking of tethered dogs, bells, the noise of someone practising with an air-rifle over towards the Zaragoza road.